by Patrick Lee

PINNACLE BOOKS   LOS ANGELES

SIX-GUN SAMURAI

An original Pinnacle Books edition, published for the first time anywhere.

First printing, November 1980

ISBN: 0-523-41190-1

Cover illustration by Bruce Minney

Printed in the United States of America

PINNACLE BOOKS, INC.
2029 Century Park East
Los Angeles, California 90067

SLICE OF DEATH . . .

"I'm talkin' to you, boy. What the hell are you doin' drinkin' in a white man's bar? Answer me, you flat-faced bastard!"

A flicker of a tight-lipped smile creased the stranger's face; his eyes were deadly black spots that bored into Frank's narrow face as he took two swift steps forward, his right hand sweeping across his body, grasping the hilt of his sword. "Long ago I was known in your country as Tommy Fletcher." The surname came out "Fretcher."

For an instant, recognition seemed to flash in Frank's eyes; some stray memory nudged at his consciousness. Then he brushed it away, unable to make a solid connection. His hand dipped to his side as he made his play. The well-oiled Remington slid smoothly from its soft pouch holster, Frank's hand closing on it, thumb drawing downward on the hammer.

Tanaka's samurai sword came out edge-upward, swinging to the right in a graceful rising arc. For an instance his face glowed with satisfaction. He released a shrill, keening cry that sounded even more frightening than a Rebel yell.

Frank felt a sharp, snapping pain in his right wrist, as though someone had jerked tight a looped piece of wire. Distracted by the unexpected sensation, he glanced downward. Horror and disbelief blanched his face pale white as he saw his gun—and hand—lying on the floor at his feet. Bright crimson spurted from the useless stump. Stunned, he dropped to his knees, his left hand clutching his right arm above the wrist.

Tanaka's *katana* continued its circular swing, far to the right, before he reversed his hold, closed palm now upward, bringing the blade back level, just above Frank's shoulder height. Frank looked up in time to see it coming. He opened his mouth to scream, but no sound came. . . .

This one is dedicated to Gaye
Tardy . . . a real sweetheart of
an editor.

AUTHOR'S NOTE

For the purpose of uniformity and simplicity for English speaking and reading persons, certain liberties have been taken with the Japanese language. For example:

Dai Nihon, the proper Japanese for Japan, is rendered here as the more familiar *Dai Nippon.*

The same is true for *Japanese,* which is used throughout in place of the proper *Nihon-ji.*

Although the Imperial Army was not fully operative along European lines regarding Table of Organization, until the late 1870s, the terms *butai* (detachment), and *rentai* (regiment), are used here in place of the longer and more difficult to pronounce words that more properly describe the Samurai *TO* during the days of the Early West.

For simplicity, also, the proper *Yedo* (EE-Ay-do) is rendered as *Edo* (Ay-do), to denote Tokyo.

Likewise, there are four names for the short, stabbing sword carried by samurai. Among them *wasizaki* was in use only during the period 1927-1945, and so it was decided to go with the most literal, *ho-tachi,* which means "small" or "short" sword.

A glossary of Japanese and Spanish terms used in this book is included in the appendix.

—Patrick Lee

PROLOGUE

Lightning flashed over the pagoda-like rooftops, dancing in writhing, demented strides from one skyward-pointing copper spike to another. Each blaze of light illuminated the wind-tortured trees which lashed about like tormented souls in hell. The electric violence extended far out over the countryside, shedding its brightness on the white-mantled slopes of that ancient symbol of maternal protection, Mount Fujiyama. Rain descended suddenly, whipped along by the gale in wave-like torrents. The fury of the storm perfectly masked the approach of a band of black-clad figures.

No lights showed in the American mission compound as the first of the dark-clothed, hooded figures reached the outer gate. He paused until others gained his position, then allowed a small smile of satisfaction to bend his thin, cruel lips. It would be easy! The ugly, foreign devils would pay for their stupidity in not posting guards and *Dai Nippon* would be purged, once and for all, of their odious presence. True, the emperor, the Son of Heaven, would lose much face over this night's work. What matter that, though, considering the huge reward offered by the *daimyo* of Osaka for ridding the sacred kingdom of these white barbarian enemies. With silent gestures, he directed his men to their tasks.

Grapnel hooks, connected to stout, slender cords, were thrown over the wall and secured. A swarm of ebony-suited men pulled their way up them and dropped silently into the muddy courtyard beyond. When the last man went over, their leader joined them. Taking the pieces from bags, slung over the shoulders of three of the party, they assembled an iron-headed,

1

brass battering ram. At another silent signal, they rushed the main door.

Wood splintered from the night bar and the hinges groaned in their sockets as the ram struck its first blow. Roused from his light slumber, the porter leaped to his feet as the second thrust boomed through the hallway. On the third attempt, the lightly secured portal sprang open. The porter's eyes widened with fear and he turned to run, his mouth opening to shriek the last word of his life.

"Ninja!"

Three *shuriken*, the five-pointed, flying stars of death, glittered in the torchlight, striking into the fleeing man's back, staggering him. The sticky, black, poisonous substance on their tips instantly started to work on his nervous system. One of his hands jerked erratically to the source of pain as the lithe, muscular leader of the raiders dashed to him. A thin ribbon of light shimmered on the keen edge of the leader's *O-tachi katana*—his great sword—while it descended in a perfect arc, striking the porter's head cleanly off his shoulders. The shouted warning had its effect, though. Lights began coming on and the noise of shouted inquiries and hurried activity filled the household.

Two blue-and-white coated marines appeared in the hallway, earing back the hammers of their short-barreled muskets. Neither man fired a shot. The first guard dropped his weapon, screaming with pain as he clawed at the thin killing needles that pierced his throat. Another cloud of *tonki*, this time in the form of leaf-bladed throwing darts, filled the air and the other marine fell to the floor, writing in agony. As resistance crumbled, the leader motioned his men forward. A whispering shuffle of their *tabi*—split-toed shoe-socks—was the only sound in the hallway as they made their way into the interior of the building.

Tommy Fletcher dozed lightly, in a state between sleep and being fully awake. He loved thunderstorms. As a small boy he used to sit at night, nose pressed to the window of his room, watching them unleash their

2

violence over the rolling hills of his family home in northern Georgia. But that had been when he was a little kid. Now, as a nearly grown-up, twelve-year-old midshipman in the United States Navy, on detached duty from Commodore Perry's flagship, he felt he must put aside such childish things. Particularly in light of his sudden elevation in status; being assigned to the newly formed American mission to this strange and exciting country of Japan.

For the time being, he contented himself with listening to the rumble of thunder while drifting in an insubstantial half-world. A smile bloomed on his face each time he recorded on his eyelids another flash of lightning. The porter's terrified shout, and the screams of the dying, jerked him rudely from his euphoric mood.

More men died shrieking and the sound of shredding lacquered tissue partitions reached his ears. A sudden chill of fear spread over Tommy's naked body. He threw back the bedcovers and hurried to the door. Sliding the lacquer-stiffened panel open only enough to peek out, he peered into the hallway. Tommy's eyes widened with the realization of the danger he faced when he saw a mob of black-clothed men swarming down the passageway toward him. He quickly shut the door and dropped the locking pin into its bottom frame. It would, he knew, buy him only seconds.

Frightened, but acting in a controlled, disciplined manner—ingrained during the long months of the cruise under Perry—the boy paused only long enough to slip into a pair of the not quite knee-length breeches favored by the Japanese commoners who worked for the mission. Tommy had taken a liking to them, along with his adopting the Japanese custom of sleeping nude, finding the loose pantaloons most comfortable on hot, humid days when his absence from duties allowed him to shed his tight-fitting, scratchy, woolen navy uniform. His purpose in donning the loose trousers was not formed from modesty so much as practicality and cool reason.

Despite the urgency of the flight he planned, Tommy took time to appraise the benefits his appearance held for him. His black hair and equally dark, shoe-button eyes, with their slight almond cast—inherited from his Cherokee ancestors—would allow him to blend into the local population, at least until he learned what had caused this sudden attack and was able to appeal his plight to representatives of the emperor, or *Mikkado*, as his subjects called him. Naked, though, the pale, untanned skin below his navel would instantly give him away, he felt. Likewise, his uniform could prove a fatal disadvantage. So he purposefully dressed in a way to let him hide among the natives. Satisfaction with this decision on his future course came as Tommy tied the cord that held up his sole piece of attire. He jumped on his bed, eyeing the translucent, white, lacquered square that comprised his window.

It would give him little resistance, Tommy thought. Flexing his knees, he sprang upward and dived through the paper pane. At the same instant the sliding door splintered inward. Tommy hit in the mud, slithering forward on his belly. Behind him he heard the voice of Anson Pearsoll, head of the mission.

"Tommy! Run! Tom Fletcher, run for your life, boy!" The kindly, gray-haired gentleman's words ended in a wetly gargling silence as the razor edge of a *katana* decapitated him.

For the first time, Tommy Fletcher gave way to emotion. A sob of desperation escaped his lips and his vision blurred with unshed tears as he forced himself to his feet. Confused and terrified now, he sloughed his way through the gummy, sucking mud.

He fell twice more before reaching the outer wall. Using a sturdy vine and hooking his toes over protrusions in the plastered, mud-block palisade, he climbed upward. Near the top, he froze in fright, feeling cold sweat break out as an arrow clattered against the surface an inch from his extended right hand. More missiles rattled nearby and he struggled to get over the top.

The boy cut his leg and stomach crawling over the wall. His injures came from the sharpened oyster shells and bits of volcanic glass imbedded in the top to discourage prowlers. Blood trickled from the slight cuts,

4

mixing with the beating rain as he dropped to the ground in a foreign and suddenly hostile city. Turning first left, then right, Tommy plunged into the darkness, running without plan or destination.

Tommy's mind spun with doubts and uncertainties as he fled sure and terrible death, seeking refuge he knew not where.

Chapter One

Glaring white sunlight, painfully bright, faded everything outside to a uniform, washed-out tan. A light breeze, seemingly created out of the rising heat waves, struggled to assemble a dust devil, failed and dropped its burden, dispersing as quickly as it had come. Not even the few bloated, black flies dared risk exertion in the stifling oppression of the one-hundred-twenty degree temperature. Moving as little and infrequently as possible, the inhabitants of Washout, Nevada endured the midday furnace, praying silently to survive until the coolness of nightfall.

Raul Sanchez, the bartender in the Golconda Saloon, was one of them. Only when one of the two men standing at the far end of the bar listlessly raised an empty glass to signal for service did he leave his perch on a high stool behind the thick, pine plank and amble slowly to a place before them. Raul didn't like his customers. Their hard, cruel faces were not so uncommon. Many who passed through the batwings had a certain coldness. But a vacancy in their eyes spoke of bandido, of that class of men—and some women, too, he allowed—who had chosen to follow the trail of voilence and death to make a living.

He had seen more than his share of their kind, and the disreputable clothes, scraggly, untrimmed hair and yellowed teeth of this pair, only added to Raul's sense of unease. All the same, a customer was a customer. At their next high sign, he slid from the stool and shuffled toward them. Raul's eyes drooped with a lethargy that infected everyone in Washout. His all but closed circle of black moustache nearly surrounded thin, *indio* lips

6

made even more meager by the protruding teeth they struggled to cover. His movements, as he raised the bottle and poured whiskey, were those of a fragile, old man. He exhibited no greater quickness, in defiance of usual custom, in reaching out to take the ten-cent pieces from in front of each man.

"*¡Que la chingada!* How can you drink that stuff in this weather?" he asked for perhaps the tenth time since the two drifters had entered the saloon. Raul didn't expect an answer, it was too hot for conversation, but he persisted in expressing his own feelings on the subject.

"*Mira,* a shot or two of tequila I can understand. It makes you sweat and cleans out the body, cools a man off. Or a *cerveza,* foamy and cold from the limestone spring in our cellar. Oh, *sí,* that I believe to benefit one such as yourself . . . or me, for that matter. *¿Por que no*? If you gentlemen will watch the—how you say, store?—I shall go and attend to that very thing." Licking his lips in thirsty anticipation, Raul departed without getting a reply.

Frank Tollar looked up at his partner. Dust begrimed their clothes and clung, in sweat-dampened clots, to their three-day stubbles of beard. Joe Coaker's gray eyes showed an irritated redness like that of an enraged bull. From the stinging, itchy discomfort he felt when he blinked, Frank knew his own must look the same. Wetting dry lips with his thick-feeling tongue, Frank curled his mouth into a sullen sneer.

"Big deal you figured out here, Joe. The colonel's not going to be too happy about it . . . and I sure ain't. Hell and tarnation. They sure named this burg right proper. Washout. It was a bust before it ever got to be a boomtown. So just tell me where and how we find all this tidy sum of money you say's layin' around here?"

"Now dang it, Frank. It was here the last time I was through. That's why I contacted Hollister an' he sent you. An' that was a little over six weeks ago. It's not my fault you took so long gettin' here. We hit a bad time, that's all. This dry spell and the heat. Most places out here, when it gets like this, they take a sie-esta, like the Mezkins. You wait 'til sundown. You're gonna see this place come alive. I mean a-live." Joe's slack lips peeled back in a wet smile, revealing his neglected, rotting teeth. He peered anxiously into Frank's mean, amber eyes.

Frank gave vent to his scorn. "A two-man job, you said. Hell, from the look of it, two eleven-year-old, wet-behind-the-ears sprats could handle it. I wouldn't want to say you were bettin' your life on this turnin' out right, Joe. Howsomever, you dragged me away from a right nice little money-making scheme the colonel had goin' over Sacramento way to help you relieve these folks of some excess gold—and I don't like makin' all these miles for nothing. I joined the gang after the War because I thought I could make out better than on my own. So, whatever we take outta here, it best impress me more'n what I've seen so far."

"Relax, Frank, relax. I'd never tell Colonel Hollister anything that weren't true. What we both need is a bath, some grub, and a little snooze. When that pepper-belly gets back from samplin' his own wares, we'll have him rustle us up some fri-holies and beef. Then a nice tub over at that barbershop and a soft bed. All we got to do after that is wait until the sun goes down and the fun begins."

Raul returned then, clutching two sweat-beaded, brown bottles. He emitted a beery belch, clinked the containers together and addressed his patrons.

"I have proven the wisdom of my words, *Señores.* And, being a wise and cautious man, I have returned with that proof to console me through this day of great tribulation."

"Yeah. Fine, fine. Now, you have any eats around here? Grub? Co–uh–*comidas?*"

Raul's face brightened. *"¡Ay, comidas, sí!"* Then he took on a look of regret. "Only it desolates me, *Señor,* to have to inform you we do not provide meals in this place. There is, of course, the *lonchería* of Maria Elena Sanchez de Gomez, who has the honor to be my sister, although misfortunate enough to be married to

8

that worthless loafer of a bum, Pablo Esteban Gomez . . ."

"Jesus! We didn't ask for a look at your family tree, hombre. All we want is some food." Joe nodded agreement with Frank's words.

Raul placed two fingers in his mouth and whistled shrilly. A barefoot boy of about ten, clad in the white, pajama-like clothes of a peon farmer, dashed in through the rear door. Both garments were cut off raggedly short, above the knees and elbows, obvious hand-me-downs. He snatched a straw sombrero off his head, clutched it in front of his chest with both hands. His black, intelligent eyes were fixed on Raul.

"¿Si, Papá?" The boy's eyes wavered, taking in the two trail-stained, mean-looking men at the bar.

"What is it you wish, Señores?"

"Some beans, tortillas, beefsteak, if there is any, coffee," Frank commanded. "And make that well done."

Raul rapidly translated the order into Spanish. Then admonished his son, "Andale, Pepito."

"¿Carne de res por los hombres malos?" Pepito asked to be sure his father truly meant to serve these gringos from their scant supply of beef.

"¡No, burro estúpido! Carne de borrego."

Pepito grinned, his eyes alight with glee. He knew most gringos didn't like mutton. That would show them.

From unknown hiding places, which afforded protection from the infernal heat of afternoon, crickets, cicadas, and frogs miraculously appeared as the sun set beyond the distant mountains. Their nocturnal chorus seemed to beckon to the human inhabitants, who started to appear, singly and in clumps, on the streets of Washout. A piano began to tinkle in a small dance hall-saloon and moments later the staccato, bell-like notes of a trumpet and excited, ringing rhythm of many guitars answered from the Golconda, where a Mariachi band was tuning up. Horses' hoofs drummed in the dusty main street and the shrill laughter of a whore came from Tillie's Crystal Palace. Frank and Joe hit the boardwalk from their hotel as the last light faded from the summer sky.

"I'll give you there's more people, Joe." Frank's grudging admission was followed by further derision. "That still don't say the money's flowin' like you said."

"Oh, no? Hell, Frank, look around you. Them girls over at Tillie's don't give it away; an' eats, likker an' cards come dear, too. Only one place you'd figure not to be open this time of day, right? The bank. Well, considerin' the upside-down way people live around here, that ain't the case. They got a nice little bank here, with a night deposit system to take care of what's taken in at all these other places. One teller and a clerk keep the door open until about an hour after closin' for the saloons and all. That's what I wrote to Colonel Hollister. So what we have to do is wait until these nice folks gather those gobs of money in one place for us and then help ourselves.

"Sorta make some kind of record, won't it? I mean, pullin' an armed robbery on a bank at midnight? Not everybody can do that, right, Frank?"

"Don't go spendin' that money until you got it in your hand, Joe." They broke stride and Frank pushed open the batwings to the Golconda. They entered and bellied up to the bar. "Beer."

"Same for me."

"We're gonna have to do some lookin' around first, Joe. Check out things. Like where's the law in this town?"

"There's an old guy who's town marshal. He'll be at home now, asleep. He's got two young deputies. They're big and strong. Work nights, of course. 'Bout the only thing they're really good for is to break up any ruckus that starts in one of the saloons or the bawdy house. One of 'em don't even carry a gun. He uses an axe handle. The other packs a Winchester. Something comes up, he cracks the feller alongside the head with that saddle gun and drags him off to the lockup. Real high toned lawmen."

"Hmmm." Frank drank deeply of his beer, wiping white traces of the head from his moustache. He

10

checked the time shown on a pendulum clock hung on the wall above the small stage where the *Mariachi* band played: eight-forty-five. It was going to be a long night. Hell! Some big things were brewin' and he was missing out on them. The rest of the gang had headed south to Arizona on a big operation Hollister had planned; and here he stood, caught up in a two-bit stickup arrangement, dreamed up by a cuss who wasn't even rightly a member of the bunch. When he joined up with the others, with little or nothing to show for it . . . He'd give the colonel a piece of his mind, don't think he wouldn't.

Beside him, Joe suddenly gave a choking guffaw, spraying beer from his mug as he set it down to dig his elbow into Frank's ribs. He continued to giggle, and nodded toward the doorway where a new arrival had entered the saloon.

"What in tarnation's got into you?" Frank turned his head to see what prompted this display of hilarity from his partner and came up short. His mouth fell open. His eyes widened in wonder. Nowhere had he ever seen anything quite like this strangely dressed man—at least he thought it was a man—who stood just inside the batwings. The man's lower extremities were clad in ordinary enough denim trousers—which had grown continually more popular since the gold rush days when Levi Strauss had first sewn them from sailcloth and dyed them blue. There, all relationship to things seen or known before stopped for Frank.

The newcomer wore over his torso a white, buttonless jacket with a long, skirted hem. It was made of a coarse material, tightly woven and lightly padded. The loose sleeves ended part-way between wrist and elbow. Twin tails of a narrow, black cord, by which he kept it closed, showed under a wide, brightly colored sash with ornate designs. The oddness didn't end there.

"What's them funny looking things on his feet?" Frank asked Joe in a soft, near-whisper. "Slippers? If they is, someone sure did a poor job of fixin' 'em up. They done sewed up the big toe in its own little compartment. My, my . . . white silk slippers. Ain't we the pretty one though."

"He sure ain't no Mezkin. Look at them wood blocks he's standin' on." Joe indicated the *gehtas* the stranger wore. "Ain't never seen no *huaraches* looked like that. Goldang! He's a big one, though, ain't he? Better'n six feet, I'd guess."

The short, stocky outlaw's eyes took in the stranger's impressive height, broad shoulders, and thick, muscular column of neck.

"Yeah, but he's sure skinny." Frank's observation made no allowance for the ample, well-corded muscles that showed in the man's forearms and at his throat. "Can you figure out what he is?"

Joe studied the newcomer's golden-tanned skin, dark hair, and black, glittering eyes, which had a slight almond shape. They contrasted confusingly with his hugeness and the long, Anglo-Saxon straightness of his nose. Full, occidental lips formed a generous, if slightly stern looking, mouth. Joe shook his head in doubt.

"If he weren't so all-fired big, I'd say he was Chinese."

"Might be, Joe. But I've never seen one so gussied up before. Mebbe some sort of coolie holiday today? An' would you look at that hairdo? Whooeee!" Frank pointed rudely at the man's hair, worn long on the sides, combed straight back, the pate shaved from forehead to back except for a topknot, held in place by a gold clasp.

"Who's he think he is with that all frizzed out in the middle of his bald spot?" Joe gave a closer look. "You think that thing holdin' it is gold, Frank?"

"That or brass. If it is gold, it'd be worth a fortune. I seed somethin' like that once in church. A picture of a Roman soldier, wearin' these bracelet things."

"You was in church?"

"Hush your fool mouth. What do you suppose he uses them sticks for?"

Frank pointed to two slightly curved, highly polished, and ornamented objects thrust into the man's wide girdle. The longer of the pair was close to five feet, while the other measured a bit over half that long. The stranger's left hand held the larger stick lightly at the

12

top of his colorful sash, while the right was draped indolently over the upper end.

Joe peered myopically a moment, took another swallow of beer. "Don't look like any cane I ever saw. Who'd ever stick their cane in their belt anyway? No matter, Frank, he ain't armed. We might as well do a little funnin' of him, huh? An' if'n that turns out to be gold, maybe we can, uh, relieve him of it?" As Joe talked on, the man walked toward the bar with a measured, unconsciously arrogant stride.

As he progressed through the room, silence followed in a rippling wave. Every man in the saloon eyed the strangely dressed man with the wary gaze of one looking upon the totally alien. The *Mariachi* music faltered and stopped in mid-phrase. When the stranger reached his destination he leaned slightly forward and spoke quietly to Raul Sanchez.

"Ichi biru, kudusai."

Raul blinked, not recognizing the foreign words.

"¿Mande? No intiendo. What itches?" When he received no reply, Raul continued again in Spanish. *"¿Por favor, habla usted Español o Ingles?"*

"Aaah, s-o-o-o. English." The words came in a breathy sibilant, near-whisper that hinted that this was a favored joke of the huge man. "So sorry, please? I want a *biru,* yes, no?" He accompanied his request with a nod toward the mug of beer still held in Frank's hand, part way between bartop and mouth."

"Oh, a *beer. Si. Momentito."*

When the frothy brew had been delivered, the man took a long, deep swallow and sat the mug on the bar. *"Dom arigato.* Thank you."

"De nada." Raul Sanchez handled the transaction with the aplomb of a man accustomed to dealing with the most outlandish of customers.

Frank and Joe exchanged glances that showed that each saw this as an opportunity for a little fun at the stranger's expense. Joe wiped the back of his hand across his mouth and threw back his head.

"Whoooeee! What kind of strange foreign critter we got here, boys?"

Frank shook his head once, as though to clear it, completed the gesture of drinking from his beer and sat the half-filled container back on the bar before answering. "Gol-dang, boys. I ain't seen me no man dressed up in a gal's skirts this side of San Francisco." Frank winked hugely at the other men in the saloon, picking up the line of rude jesting. He turned toward the oddly dressed man and raised his voice, as many are accustomed to do when addressing a foreigner.

"You Chinee-boy, ha? You workee lail-load?" Several men glanced from Frank to the stranger and back again, then cleared the space between them. They sensed, from long experience, that the funning would soon turn nasty. The foreigner remained silent, ignoring Frank, looking intently at his beer mug.

"Hey, boy! I askee you, look-see, chop-chop. You workee sumbitch darkee mine, huh? You lan'lee boy, washee clothes . . . no tickee, no lan'lee, yes?"

The man slowly, deliberately finished his beer. He still did not raise his eyes to look at Frank Tollar. Frank's face flushed and sudden fury sounded warningly in his voice.

"I'm talkin' to you, boy. What the hell are you doin' drinkin' in a white man's bar? Answer me, you flat-faced, Chink bastard!"

A flicker of a tight-lipped smile creased the stranger's face. He breathed in deeply and exhaled in a suppressed sigh. Then he stepped clear of the bar. When he looked up, his eyes had gone flat, deadly, black spots that bored into Frank's narrow face. The man's mouth turned hard and cruel. His lips writhed like muscular snakes, as though he found it distasteful to address anyone so inferior as the pigeon-breasted creature with the lank, greasy, blond hair who had insulted him.

"A wise man once said that it is most foolish for one to attack a force whose strength and position he does not know. It is unfortunate that the military master, a former *daimyo* of Osaka, who spoke this wisdom three hundred years ago did not heed his own advice. He died at the battle of *Sekigehara*, which made Tokugawa

14

Iyeyasu *Sei-e-tai Shōgun* over *Dai Nippon*. A Tokugawa-san held that position until Emperor Meijis succession five years ago.

"It is likewise unfortunate that you have not the breeding or intelligence to keep your mongrel mouth closed in the presence of your betters. I am Tanaka Ichimara Tomi of the *Fujika* samurai *rentai,* former Master of Horse to the shogun and Standard Bearer."

Frank Tollar flushed a deeper red, to the roots of his long, stringy blond hair. Spittle formed in the corners of his thin-lipped mouth and flew wildly as he shouted. "I don't give a damn if you're the king of this here Nippon! No flat-faced, Chinee sumbitch talks to me like that and lives!"

"*¡Señor . . . señor! . . .* He has no gun." In the same moment Raul Sanchez sought to warn Frank, his hand reached under the bar, grasping the heavy mallet used as a bung starter. He brought it out, gripping it tightly.

Tanaka took two swift steps forward, his right hand sweeping across his body, grasping the hilt of his sword. "Long ago, I was known in your country as Tommy Fletcher." The surname came out, "Fretcher."

For an instant, recognition seemed to flash in Frank Tollar's eyes, some stray thread of memory nudging at his consciousness. Then he brushed it away, unable to make a solid connection. His hand dipped to his side as he made his play. The well-oiled Remington slid smoothly from its soft pouch holster, Frank's hand closing on it, thumb drawing downward on the hammer. Then a bright ribbon of light seemed to dance before his eyes, surprise freezing him for an instant as the "stick" became a glittering, deadly tool. Tanaka further paralyzed him with a shrill, keening cry that sounded even more frightening than a Rebel yell.

Tanaka's samurai sword came out edge-upward, swinging to the right in a graceful, rising arc. For an instant, his face glowed with satisfaction.

Frank Tollar felt a sharp, snapping pain in his right wrist, as though someone had jerked tight a looped piece

15

of wire. Distracted by the unexpected sensation, he glanced downward. Horror and disbelief blanched his face pale white as he saw his gun . . . and hand lying on the floor at his feet. Bright crimson spurted from the useless stump. Stunned, he dropped to his knees, left hand clutching his arm above the right wrist.

Tanaka's *katana* continued its circular swing, far to the right, before he reversed his hold, closed palm now upward, bringing the blade back level, just above Frank's shoulder height. Frank looked up in time to see it coming. He opened his mouth to scream, but no sound came.

For a fraction of a second, Frank felt triumph. The dumb slant-eyes had missed. He still had a chance. He sent his left arm a command to draw the police model, converted Colt, tucked into his waistband with the butt to the front. But his arm wouldn't obey. Tanaka changed position, legs wide-spread, arms over his head, holding his weapon high in a two-hand grip. Frank's vision blurred as he watched this and he shook his head in exasperation at this turn of events.

That's when his head fell backward off his neck to dangle between his shoulder blades by a narrow strip of flesh. Twin fountains of blood geysered toward the ceiling from his severed carotid arteries and Frank's body did a brief, gruesome dance of death before falling to the floor. Tanaka ignored the corpse, advancing on Joe Coaker.

That's one down, Tanaka thought exultantly. *But where are the others? They were supposed to be riding together.*

"Hey, friend, I don't want no trouble with you," Joe whined all the while his hand slid cautiously toward the butt of his holstered Colt Frontier .44 revolver. Tanaka's sword descended again, swinging sideways once more. Joe felt a fleeting flash of sharp pain, followed almost at once by a strange tingling sensation running up his right arm and the tap-tap . . . tap-tap sound of his fingers hitting the floor.

"Then we make certain of it, yes?"

Joe screamed and fell to his knees, clutching at his

16

bleeding, useless right hand. Several saloon girls had been shrieking in terror from the time Frank's head fell off and now other voices joined theirs in frantic yells.

The batwings flew open and two burly, broad-shouldered men entered. One held an axe handle at the ready while the other swung a Winchester "Yellow Boy" saddle carbine in one ham-huge fist. They advanced on Tanaka, who once more held the *ichi-do*, on-guard position, legs spread, sword vertically in front of him, both hands on the hilt, held on a level with his navel. A quick glance from both men apprised them of the situation. They moved in swiftly and the deputy with the axe handle made a swing.

Bright, naked steel flashed and the axe handle lost six inches of length. Tanaka had no desire to harm those whom he recognized as being the authorities, but he intended to protect himself from harm long enough to end the combat and explain what had happened. As he shifted his attention to the other man, he saw the deputy with the rifle start to bring it up to his shoulder. Tanaka took a step backward then and changed the position of his sword.

That's when Raul Sanchez swung the bung starter with all his might.

Chapter Two

Tanaka Ichimara Tomi came to in the jail. The facility actually served most of the time as a storage shed built between the small building that housed the town clerk and marshal's office and a dry goods store.

It was made of adobe, with narrow, barred windows high in the rear wall. The cell portion was separated from the surplus merchandise by a wall of iron bars that bisected the room, front to rear. Tanaka opened his eyes to the rhythm of a fiercely pounding headache.

He had been struck from behind. That much he knew and cursed himself for it. A good samurai would never allow that to happen. The shipboard inactivity and nearly constant travel since arriving had taken the edge off his finely honed reflexes and wary sense of danger. No doubt the harmless looking Mexican bartender had been responsible, thought Tanaka. Yet he'd never seen a weapon. Fine start he had made on his mission, he chided himself, with sour acceptance of his present confinement. Only one man accounted for, the others still free to go as they wish. And here he sat in a cell.

From the beginning, when he received General Tomlinson's letter, he had accepted the possibility that the end result of his acts might well be imprisonment or execution. Under the code of *bushido*, the demands of honor and vengeance made that unimportant. His family . . . and what had happened to them . . . came first. It was a samurai's duty to avenge wrong against a blood kin. Funny, Tanaka thought as the headache lessened in severity. Although he clearly recalled his childhood in Georgia, and life before the raid on the mis-

18

sion, he now thought of himself as more Japanese than American. . . .

Tommy Fletcher had wandered the streets of *Edo* for three weeks, cold, hungry, and for the most part, unnoticed. He had a sharp, inquiring mind and quick ear for languages. He'd learned passable Spanish from the mess boys the commodore had obtained in the Philippine Islands, during the short, two-week journey from Luzon to the Isles of Nippon.

Necessity now tutored him in Japanese. Within a few days, he was able to beg for *cha* (tea), *gohan* (boiled rice), and *yasai tenpura no-tomo* (fried vegetables) in return for work. Although his once-flat belly seemed always to be swollen from the quantities of rice he put away each day, he experienced constant hunger pangs. The dietary habits of his Western upbringing made his body cry out for meat. Only the upper classes, though Tommy didn't know it at the time, had thrown off the prohibitions of Buddhism and returned to the eating of meat permitted under Shinto, the state religion.

Thus, when he was able to exchange a few hours of exhausting labor, hauling at fishnets or helping unload fishing boats laden with *kaki* (oysters), *ise ebi* (lobster), and other seafood, his reward only infrequently included a scrap of fish, squid, or octopus. Never any red flesh. More often, he had to try to satisfy the aching demands of heavily exercised, growing muscles with vegetables and rice. On his twenty-third day at large in the sprawling city of Tokyo—*Edo* as the natives called it—Tommy received part of his payment in a treasure he considered far greater than anything he'd had before.

As he left the spindly shack of an ancient, gray-haired fisherman, for whom he had worked several times, Tommy clutched in one hand a cloth headband that contained three shrimp-stuffed rice balls. In his other tightly clenched fist he held four pieces of *buton*. Made of powdered rice, sugar, and the syrup of tiny, sour plums, the *buton* candy represented the first sweets he had encountered since the midnight raid of

19

the Ninjas on the American mission, and his hurried flight to escape being murdered.

"Dom arigato gasiamashita, Obu-san." Tommy bowed low, as he had seen others do, thanking the old man with the greatest formality, properly fitting the position of an inferior to one of greater rank, and addressing the aged fisherman as tradition required as, "Honored Grandfather."

The old man, with equal gravity, told Tommy he was welcome, then added, with a warm chuckle, *"kiku-san."* Although he had heard the term, Tommy had never been addressed as "little sir" before. The kindness seemed almost as great to him as the extra food and candy treat, which had been presented to him following the evening meal—the only compensation Tommy had expected for his day-long efforts straining at the nets.

Soaking wet all the time, in and out of the water repeatedly to unsnarl the fragile strands, Tommy had worked the nets naked, as did all the other fishing fleet boys. Constant exposure to the sun had given him an overall golden hue that made it nearly impossible to distinguish him from Japanese children of his age. Only his height, nearly as large as an adult Japanese, set him apart. Although he still harbored remnants of typically Western feelings of impropriety at so much public nudity—something the Japanese accepted with casual indifference—Tommy felt his changed appearance provided added protection. He had yet to find some way to reach officials of the court so he appreciated this and tolerated his frequent nakedness.

For his own part, though, he could still not understand why, after being in the water all day, he was expected to take a scalding hot bath each evening before the one meal of the day. Aboard Commodore Perry's ship, regulations had required a once-a-week sluicing down in the scuppers for all hands. Shivering as the cold sea water washed over him from the pumps, his naked, bony shanks exposed to the eyes of the entire crew, Tommy had endured it along with the others. To him, however, that had seemed an excessive and unhealthy interest in bathing.

Once on his own in Edo, he seen discovered that the Japanese, regardless of age or sex, were throwing off their clothes and getting into water of some sort at every opportunity. Although he quickly became aware he felt better for following the custom——had never even suffered the sniffles——and no longer had a sour smell about his body, Tommy could not quite bring himself to admit the source of these benefits. Even as he left the old fisherman's shack, rejoicing in his improved status——which included an invitation to return the next day for more work——the thought would never have occurred to the boy that his new acceptance was because he had become, and smelled, more Japanese.

He would have been even more surprised to learn that the old man realized Tommy was white. Although he ascribed Tommy's poor command of the language and customs to his belief that the boy was a runaway child of the *Ainu*, never suspecting him to be a foreign devil. The *Ainu*, Caucasian-looking Japanese, inhabited the farthest north island and were a part of the "untouchable" class of Nippon; the butcherers of livestock and gatherers and buriers of the dead. But a twelve-year-old, suddenly cast onto his own resources in a foreign and hostile land, didn't question the first really full belly and show of affection he had received. Tommy's pleasure in his new circumstances ended when he rounded the first corner.

Spread out in a loose semicircle that covered the narrow, cobbled street, a mob of waifs blocked Tommy Fletcher's path. Scavengers who made their way in the same manner Tommy had discovered, they prowled the waterfront day and night to feed themselves. They had long ago banded together and were quick to resent the presence of any newcomer who represented a corresponding drop in their meager income. The nominal leader wasted no time in making their position clear.

"Aaah so-o-o. The filthy *Ainu* boy who has robbed us of work and food. What have you in that cloth to share with us?"

Startled, and more than a little uneasy, Tommy made a hesitant reply. "Wha-I . . . Only what I worked for."

21

A chorus of jeers rose from the ring of boys. "You lie! Ishu and Hiro watched you eat with the old man and then take even more food away with you. That is the same as stealing it from our bellies. Now you will give it to us!" The boys moved forward menacingly.

A chill breeze off the bay, and a slight bit of apprehension, sent a tingling shudder through the bare flesh of Tommy's chest and back. He had no real fear of any of these boys. Although of his own age and older, they were all smaller than he. Taking on any two or three at a time, he felt confident he could whip them. He had been forced to do so before. Yet together, they represented a real threat. He took a step backward and, when he saw the others hesitate an instant, committed himself.

Dropping his headband with the rice balls, Tommy began swinging. Closing with them, using feet and fists, knees and elbows, Tommy fought his way through the ring of shouting, struggling youngsters. He flung one small boy into two others, punched the leader solidly in the nose, and found himself beyond their cordon. He turned back and tried to fight his way to the precious food he had left behind.

One of the boys snatched the headband from the ground and ran, while three others formed a rear guard. Tommy charged after them. He knocked one boy sprawling, tripped over the tangle of legs and arms and surged to his feet to continue pursuit. Loudly yelling insults, his adversaries disappeared around a corner with Tommy on their heels.

Head down, Tommy dashed into the next street to collide with a pair of sturdy, silk kimono-clad legs. Rebounding, Tommy looked up into the stern face of a samurai. The boy's anger turned to eye-widening fear as he took a staggering step backward. One of the first lessons he had learned when he went into hiding among the common people was that the samurai had almost godlike power over those of lesser status. On occasion, when angered or offended, they killed with impunity. Now Tommy found himself responsible for nearly

22

bowling one of these arrogant warriors off his feet. The boy's lips trembled as he tried to form an apology.

"I . . . I-I-I-I'm s-sorry, Honorable Sir."

"So-o-o. What is this? A small rat escaped from some ship, no doubt. One that has muddied my kimono and nearly knocked me from my feet. Not to mention, offending my dignity enormously. We pay children a one *sen* copper for every rat they kill. Is there any reason I should let you live? *Wakarimasu desu?*"

Tommy understood little of it though his utterly real conviction he would die in a second carried meaning of its own. It also prevented him from hearing the slight note of humor in the knight's voice. He tried to form words in Japanese to make reply, stammering as he spoke.

The samurai reached out suddenly, grabbing Tommy by his arm, hurting him with the grip of his powerful fingers. "Speak clearly, boy! No son of Nippon should butcher his language like that."

Hearing this pronouncement, Tommy felt a glowing fragment of hope. "*Iei Amerika-jin.*"

Recoiling as though he'd been struck a violent blow, the samurai sucked air through his teeth in the Japanese manner of showing surprise. "*Amerika-jin?*"

"*Hai.*"

"*Fukanō!*" He repeated himself, "But that is impossible. All of the barbarians died in the attack on their mission." The warrior-knight's eyes narrowed and he shook Tommy effortlessly, as he would a rag toy. "Speak truthfully, boy, or you will suffer for it."

Quickly, carefully as he could with his limited Japanese, Tommy explained about his escape from the slaughter in the compound. When the death blow he expected did not come, Tommy went on to tell of his weeks on the streets. Through it all, the samurai's face remained impassive. When Tommy finished he felt he had done nothing to save himself. He lowered his chin on his chest, eyes brimming with unshed tears.

"And these ruffians who ran around me like a swarm of lice? Are you with them?"

Another reprieve, Tommy's mind registered. "No, sir. I . . . I fought them and was chasing them."

"Aa-h, so-o-o. One against so many? You have spirit, I'll say that."

The words gave Tommy even more courage. Blinking away the tears, he lashed out with a bare foot, kicking the samurai in the shin. "I'll not let you kill me, either! Not without a fight."

Instead of the whispering slither of unsheathing steel that Tommy knew would mark his departure from this earth, he heard low, growling laughter. "Spirit to spare from the looks of it." The samurai shoved Tommy out to arm's length. "Here, boy, I am not going to kill you. Dry your eyes and look at me."

Embarrassed, Tommy didn't realize he'd been crying. He raised his eyes, wiping them with a bare arm, to find a beaming smile on the samurai's face. Surprise ebbed and he tried a flickering attempt at returning a shy grin. The samurai spoke again.

"I am Tanaka Nobunara, in the service of the shogun, Tokugawa-san, and the emperor. *Anata no onamae wa?*"

"T-Tommy. Tommy Fletcher."

"Ah! Good, Tommy *Fretcher*. Let's take you home and clean you up. Perhaps you can prove an advantage to the shogun and our emperor."

"What do you mean?" Tommy's boldness came from the sudden relief that poured through his body.

"Hmmm. I suppose you would not know. The emperor, and my master, the shogun, lost much face after accepting the American mission here in Edo and the trading factors at Shimoda and Hakodate harbors, then having them wiped out to the last man. Although they had nothing to do with that, it is said they should have prevented it. Perry is to return next year and it will be up to the shogun to explain these things to him . . . and perhaps expiate the government's lost face through honorable *seppuku*.

"I am a simple man and do not understand politics, but something tells me that with you alive, able to tell what happened, the daimyo of Osaka will not be quite

24

so overbearing at court and the emperor may be able to make amends to your country, without offering my master's death. So. That is enough. Come with me."

Tommy Fletcher never became a tool of international power politics. Policy advisors in the shogun's office counseled against the wisdom of admitting that a child had survived, one who had been forced by circumstances to live as an urchin and had not been afforded the protection of the Imperial government. That left Tommy in the custody of Tanaka Nobunara.

To further complicate matters regarding one Thomas James Fletcher, midshipman, U.S. Navy, when Perry returned to Japan the next year, 1854, he employed his own form of power politics. Learning of the destruction of the mission had greatly angered the sailor-diplomat. He decided, after discovering who was believed to be responsible, on a show of force. Perry set sail for Osaka with two steam frigates in company with his flagship. The vessels were all armed with the recently developed Parrot rifles, a breech-loading, rifled-barrel cannon.

When Perry stood off the Osaka roads, the daimyo ordered his artillery to fire on the American ships. In a twenty-minute-long gun duel between three naval units of the U.S. Navy and the heavy batteries of Osaka castle, the results didn't speak well for *Dai Nippon*. The fortress castle, considered impregnable for over four hundred years, was totally destroyed. Resultant fires started in the city reduced Osaka to ashes. Perry made his point and diplomatic relations were firmly established without the presence of Tommy Fletcher. Which still left the boy's future undecided.

During that time, Tommy continued to live and study as a child of the samurai class in the home of Tanaka Nobunara. For the seven years of their marriage, the samurai's principal wife had remained childless, which deprived Tommy of close companions, but made his presence cherished by the young couple. One evening, following their usual communal bath in the huge, steaming, family-size wooden tub that sat above ground in the yard behind the house, Tanaka came to Tommy, asking if the boy would take a stroll with him in the formal gardens to the rear of the residence. Once isolated among the graceful, stunted trees, shrubs, and ornately created rock designs, Tanaka made Tommy a proposition.

"It does not look as though you shall see your homeland for a long time . . . if ever. A boy needs a family to grow properly. It would make Joshi and I most happy if you would become *musuko* . . . our son. We have no other children. Under our laws," he rushed to explain to the gape-mouthed boy before Tommy could make any reply but the desired one, "that would give you the same status as our first-born. It may be that our ancestors are angry with us and we may never have a child. In such case, since I have no other wives and may never, the house of Tanaka would be without an heir. If you consent, this could not happen. What do you say, *Tomi*?"

Tanaka Nobunara had liked the boy's name from the first. A student of the classic poetry of ancient times, the young samurai knew that the foreign name, Tommy, had the same sound as an archaic word, that was pronounced "Tomi," which, in the old language, meant "strength of heart." It fitted the boy well, he thought. His expectations were not dampened when Tommy made his answer.

"That is more honor than I deserve, sir. I . . . If you wish it, though, I can only say . . . *hai* . . . *chichi* . . . yes, father."

Overjoyed, Nobunara crushed Tommy to his chest, embracing him warmly and holding his face so the boy could not see the tears of gratitude and love that ran from his eyes down that forbidding samurai visage.

So, Tommy Fletcher became Tanaka Ichimara (first born) Tomi and from that day forward was raised as a future samurai. . . .

A key rattled in the lock of the central partition's gate-like cell door, bringing Tanaka's attention back to the present. A thick-waisted, gray-haired man entered. His pistol holster, Tanaka noticed, was empty. The man wore a star-shaped badge on his vest and carried a tray with two cups of steaming coffee and a cloth-covered plate.

"You're awake, I see," he greeted bluffly. "I'm Hiram Oakes, the marshal. Thought you might like a bit to eat and some coffee."

"Thank you. The . . . the coffee sounds good."

Marshal Oakes extended one cup and placed the tray on a small table in the corner, taking the other mug for himself. He drew up a crudely made chair and sat studying his prisoner. A few minutes of silence passed while they both sipped their coffee. Finally the marshal shook his head as though in disbelief.

"Sanchez says that just before he popped you with that bung starter you claimed to be an American."

"That's right. Before my life in Japan, I was called Thomas Fletcher."

Oakes made a long face. "Well, then. I'd suggest you started usin' that name again. Folks around these parts don't take kindly to foreigners . . . particularly oriental ones."

Tanaka's lips formed a humorless smile, his face rigid in the haughty superiority of a samurai. "Since 1603, until Commodore Perry's arrival at Edo twenty years ago, Japan was under the Act of Exclusion, which forbade the presence of foreign white devils and other barbarians in the empire. Had Perry never landed in Japan and broken the compact, I would not have now become a foreigner in my own country. As a result, though, I have been a foreigner in one place or another since the age of twelve. Never mind the story behind that, it's much too long to go into under these circumstances." Tanaka looked meaningfully at his surroundings.

"You're not under arrest, you understand. We put you here more for your own protection, you see. Folks are mighty stirred up about what happened at the Golconda."

"I acted in defense of my person. My understanding was that this is acceptable under your laws."

"So it is, so it is. And so you did. It isn't so much what you did. That's why you aren't under arrest. It's

. . . how you did it. The man you killed—his name was Frank Tollar by the way—was a no-good, an outlaw, and probably no loss. But . . . people ain't used to seein' a gunslick like Tollar get sliced up by a big knife. They sure don't know what to think, him gettin' done in like that after makin' his draw. With one like him, it's usually the other feller's funeral they're goin' to."

"It wasn't a knife, marshal. I used a sword."

"Funniest lookin' sword I ever seen. I was with Jeb Stuart an' they never gave us any sword looked like that."

"It is a *katana*, a samurai sword. The warrior class—I suppose here you would call us knights—of Japan carry them."

"And I gather those outlandish clothes go with the sword?"

"In a way. Although I don't usually wear battle dress unless I have need of it."

"Well . . . ah . . . right. Even so, they didn't do anything toward winning you friends in this town."

"They are comfortable and serviceable. However, if the appearance of my clothes accounts in part for my being here, your suggestion to change is one I would be willing to accept."

Marshal Oakes frowned. He wasn't used to having men in his jail talk to him as though they were in charge. He decided to let it go.

"Fine. Fine, young feller. Now, somethin' you said a minute ago interests me. You say you only wear that get-up when you've got some fightin' to do. You mean to tell me you came here lookin' for some sort of trouble?"

"No trouble to anyone else but the man I sought and myself."

"Meaning Frank Tollar?"

"Formerly, Sergeant Frank Tollar, of the 251st Ohio."

Marshal Oakes's eyebrows raised questioningly. "You better explain that some."

"All right, marshal. I think some background is in

28

order. A samurai is a member of a class apart from all others in Japan. He is not of royal birth, though he often reaches noble rank and is always more than a mere soldier. He is a knight in the pay of one or another noble, but rarely a person of lesser rank than daimyo of the third class . . . sort of the equivalent of an English duke. The noble I served was the shogun, sort of the emperor's right hand. I was second, only to my adopted father, Tanaka Nobunara, in service to him."

"Seems you're a pretty important feller."

"I might have been considered so in Japan. There, my own rank was that of daimyo of the fourth class. Here I am, as you pointed out, plain Thomas Fletcher."

"Okay, Tom. Get on with your story."

Tanaka sighed heavily. "Some months ago, through diplomatic channels, I learned that my real family, my blood kin, had been murdered by a band of marauders who raided in the wake of Sherman's march through Georgia."

Oakes raised a hand in protest. "But that would have been more'n eight years ago."

Tanaka's look clearly said he hadn't expected the marshal to understand . . . or to interrupt. "I was raised, from the age of twelve, in the ways of *bushido*, the warrior's code of Japan. Under that code, such an insult—or perhaps I'd better say, offense—demands immediate and deadly response. To put it simply, I came here to get vengeance."

"If he was a Yankee sergeant, how's Tollar tie into this?"

"I'm getting ahead of myself. Let me tell it my own way. When I returned to this country, to my family's home near Wentworth, Georgia, on the Savannah River, I got little cooperation from the Reconstruction Scalawags. I had come in response to a letter sent to me by a former neighbor, General Tomlinson, who had taken the Union side. I learned from him that my mother and sister, after being raped repeatedly, had both been sabred to death . . . hacked to pieces actually. I had a little brother I'd never seen. He was near the same age then that I was when I went to Japan with

Perry. He'd been decapitated and misused in an unnatural way. My father had been tortured and hanged. All the buildings on our small plantation had been ransacked and burned. Coming from the South, I'm sure you are familiar with such things." The marshal nodded. "The ones who did it, I also discovered from General Tomlinson, were believed to be under the command of a Union infantry officer. Have you heard the name Edward Hollister? He might be calling himself Colonel Hollister?"

"Hmmm. No, can't say I have."

"From army records provided by the general through our . . . er, Japanese envoy in Washington City, I learned that Hollister served with Sherman during his march through Georgia. Something happened, I haven't yet found out what, that put Hollister at odds with the Union Army. He became one of the Bummers. That's where Tollar comes in. Some time after the fall of Atlanta, Tollar deserted from his own regiment and fell in with the 251st Ohio. A lot of men changed regiments in that informal manner as I understand it. Eventually, Tollar joined Hollister's raids. One story that I learned, that came out of the war, is that Hollister liked to use his sabre. Although eight years have passed since their deaths, I intend to hunt down those responsible.

"I now have information that Hollister is suspected of being the brains behind a large and powerful gang, made up of scum from both sides in the recent war. Tollar was with him then . . . and now. It is unfortunate I had to kill him before I could question him. Now I must find the others to get the truth."

"And . . . get revenge?"

"Yes."

A few seconds passed in silence, then the marshal stood, reaching for Tanaka's coffee cup. "I'll get us some more, Tom. Eat that sandwich, you look like you could use it."

Blazing heat once more poured from a relentless sun, stifling all activity in Washout when Tanaka Tom left the jail. He walked across the faded, warped boardwalk and placed his possessions, which Marshal Oakes had brought from the hotel to his office, in two large parfleche attached to the saddle of a pack mule tied at the hitchrail. Tanaka Tom turned back to wave at the marshal, who stood in the shade of his doorway, then swung into the saddle of a stoutly built, handsome, blooded Morgan stallion. From his clothes, flat-crowned, gray hat, flannel shirt, leather vest, Levis, and glove-soft boots, it was obvious he would be traveling for some time as Tom Fletcher.

They're out there somewhere, he thought as he rode down the baking street of Washout. *Hollister and his scum are still alive. Maybe they're holed up somewhere, or butchering more innocent people. No matter. I'll find them . . . I'll find them.*

Chapter Three

Angry, hate-filled eyes watched Tom Fletcher's progress out of town.

Joe Coaker sat in a narrow, dingy hotel room, overlooking the main drag of Washout, nursing his maimed right hand. His smoldering anger gave the small gunslinger new purpose in life. Somehow he had to find a way to revenge himself on the strange, tall young man with that terrible sword. A low growl formed in Joe's throat as Fletcher's broad-shouldered frame grew smaller in the distance. Then a new thought assailed him.

If he were to get this . . . Fletcher . . . get him good, why he could take the story of what happened to him and Frank to Colonel Hollister. Maybe then Hollister would show his gratitude by taking him into the gang. Joe's thoughts broke off abruptly and he hurled an empty whiskey glass against the far wall. What use would a fingerless gunhand be to anyone?

He looked at the heavy bandages that swathed his disfigured right hand, each stub still tinted pink. He'd learn to use his left hand. Yeah. That was it. He'd have to if he set out to even the score with this Tom Fletcher. A left-handed gunhawk. Hmmm. The idea appealed to him. He'd find Hollister, or some of his men, and tell them what he intended, then set out to do it. Sure. Easy. All he had to do was find Hollister.

Birds chirped brightly in the few trees that struggled for existence in the wash. Here, on the eastern slope of the Mogollon Rim, the pines had given over to a few hearty manzanita and scrub oak, an occasional paloverde, its short, slender leaves like a pale green mist. The steady, rhythmic chink of picks striking rock didn't disturb the feathered creatures. Over the past few months, since word spread throughout Arizona of the gold strike, they'd become used to it. Cocking their heads, first one way then the other, they looked down on the scene below with bright, black, curious eyes.

Large, floppy, dust-coated hats protected the heads of the miners, laboring to wrest the precious yellow metal from the stubborn mountain. Shirtless, the sleeves of their red longjohns rolled up, sweat making great stains at their armpits, at the small of their backs, and on their lean, hard bellies, the men toiled with single-minded purpose. Every few moments, the work was interrupted by a triumphant cry.

"Whoooeee! Lookie here, Jason. See? See? Bigger'n a goober pea. We're on the right track, you can bet."

Jason joined the excited miner, examining his find. "Man, you're pickin' at trifles. When Bob lets go that charge, we're gonna expose the whole vein. Wait and see, ya hear?"

Off at a little distance, among a cluster of patched, sun-faded Sibley tents—purchased surplus from the army depot at Fort Apache—activity of another sort continued in the lazy afternoon. Two women, stout and slightly graying, though hardly along in years enough to justify it, bent over galvanized tubs of steaming water. Their work-reddened fingers sought diligently to drub the red-orange soil from their men's clothes on the ripple-surfaced metal faces of two washboards. Nearby, three small children, the oldest about ten, scampered about as close to naked as Christian modesty would allow. Perspiration glistened on their sun-bronzed bodies as they raced in pursuit of a small lizard. As the women struggled to dislodge the stubborn dirt from flannel shirts and often-patched trousers, they talked of the one subject that occupied all their minds.

"You think Bob will do it this time, Clara? Really do it?"

"Sure as my faith in the Lord, Rita-Mae. Why, we've got near onto five hundred dollars worth o' gold so far

33

an' that's from only scratchin' the surface. Three months work now and that vein can't be much further away. Y'all mark my words. When that man of mine lets off the explosive this time, we're gonna be rich."

"Fire in the hole!" Bob Gower's lusty bellow came, and was picked up and echoed by Jason Carver. Clara Gower broke off her washing to call to the children.

"Bobby Lee, you an' them kids get down now, ya hear?"

The cotton-topped ten-year-old shouted shrilly to his younger companions and they hit the dirt. Expectant tension seized everyone at the mining claim. Silence held for several heart beats; even the birds ceased their constant twittering.

Then the powder went off.

A great gout of reddish dust mushroomed into the air, while in the same instant a loud blast rolled and rebounded off the hills, redoubling itself like brooding thunder as it dissipated in the distance. One of the washtubs jolted from its rickety stand by the following shock wave, and rock cascaded down from the face of the mountain. More dust plumed up from the falling debris and, as it clattered away down the slope, silence returned. For a moment, everyone remained motionless, dazed, their hearing dulled in the tremendous avalanche of sound. Slowly, the men rose to their feet.

"D'ya think you might have used a tad bit too much powder, Bob?"

Bob Gower studied his work, a look of concentration slowly dissolving into one of excited victory. "No, Al. No, I can't say I do. Lookie there at that." Bob pointed to the exposed strata.

Running at a drunken angle, better than two feet wide and the entire length of the blasted out area, a vein of dull red-yellow glowed in the sun. Gleaming pinpoints of brightness flashed from the quartz crystals mingled in the rich deposit. Jublilation overcame the miners. Clasping arms about each other's shoulder, they began to dance around in a frenzy.

"We did it! We did it. By God, we struck it rich!" Al Bartlett broke off his jubilant shout to dash to his wife. He lifted Rita-Mae high off her feet and twirled her around. "Oh, Honey Pie, we done found the mother lode. We're gonna be rich as Midas."

"Maw! Maw! Is it gold? Is it real gold?" Bobby Lee rushed up to cling to his mother's apron, eyes shining with excitement.

Unbidden, a small frown creased Clara Gower's brow, but she brushed away the unwanted omen of trouble with a smile. "Yes, son. It's *real* gold."

"We better get into Globe and record this," Jason advised soberly once the others had calmed down a little. "We can take in what we've got, buy equipment, more powder. Boys, we're sittin' on top of our fortunes. What say we pack up right now? We'll leave for town at first light tomorrow."

The others nodded agreement, soberly considering the immensity of what they'd uncovered. Slowly, timidly at first, the birds returned, venturing first one chirp, then a second, and third, finally a chorus, sounding as pleased with events as the two-legged creatures below their secure perches.

Four days later, Jason and Bob Gower returned from Globe. Jason was first to notice that something wasn't right. He reined in short on the top of the last ridge that separated them from their camp.

"What's the matter, Jason? Figured you'd be all-fired anxious to get back."

"Don't you hear it? I mean, don't you *not* hear it?"

Bob Gower removed his hat, scratched his head. "Hear what? I don't hear nothin' a-tall."

"That's what I mean. The birds . . . they ain't singing."

Bob frowned darkly. "You think there's trouble?"

"Could be."

"Injuns?"

"Don't know 'til we look. But we gotta be careful . . . slip up on that brow and get ourselves a look-see."

Quietly, the men dismounted, ground-reining their horses. Taking their Spencer carbines, they hunkered low and worked their way to the top of the ridge. Peer-

35

ing over, they looked down on the mine site. Nothing moved around the dun-colored tents and they saw no sign of Al or the women and children.

"Looks all right. But where you suppose everyone is? Takin' a sie-esta, maybe?"

"Could be. How about them horses down there?"

"Least it ain't 'Paches. Those saddles say white men."

"Hmmm. That could be worse than Apaches. Let's ride on in." As they returned to their mounts, Jason added as an afterthought, "Might be wise we keep our hands to these repeaters, eh?"

A few minutes later, saddle guns across their knees, each man leading a heavily laden pack animal, Bob and Jason rode down onto the flat before the tents. As they approached a tall, slender man threw back a tent flap and stepped into the open. His left hand fingered one of Bobby Lee's small shirts, while the right held a cocked Colt Frontier.

"Welcome back, gents."

"Who are you, mister?"

"Name's Turner. Pike Turner, if it means anything to you. Why don't you put them irons in their scabbards and step down?"

"What are you doing with my son's shirt?" Bob Gower demanded with sudden anger.

Turner quirked a half-smile and grunted a short, almost simpering laugh. "We were tryin' to figure out who belonged to which. Thank you. As to this shirt . . ." Turner raised his arm, gesturing toward Bob Gower with the limp piece of cloth. "Well, you might say we just wanted to make it clear who is in charge here and give you some idee of what the penalty might be if'n you don't behave."

"By God, I'll . . ."

"You'll put them damned guns away and do as you're told." Icy steel edged the whiplash of Turner's voice. He turned slightly, calling over his shoulder. "Bring 'em out, boys."

Three men emerged, herding the women and children. The youngsters turned tear-stained, anxious faces on the two mounted men. Then a fourth hardcase appeared in the opening of the other tent, shoving a beaten and bloody Al Bartlett in front of him. Al staggered and moved like a drunken man, crossing to stand beside his wife, Rita-Mae. Silence held for a while until a broken sob came from Clara Gower.

"Oh, Bob. I . . . we . . . it wasn't Al's fault. They came on us so sudden."

Bob Gower thought he recognized two of the claim jumpers as men he'd seen in the saloon at Globe. They must have ridden hard to beat them to the mine. Reluctantly he sheathed his Spencer carbine. Beside him, Jason followed suit. In the silence, the two smaller children began sniffling again.

"Now . . . down!" Pike Turner commanded. Resigned, both men complied. One of the outlaws led away the livestock. "Fine, gents," Turner went on. "We have a simple little matter to attend to. Nothing difficult." From a shirt pocket he produced a folded paper.

"This here is a legal doc-u-ment. It's an assignment paper. All you gotta do is sign it, turning over all claim and interest in this here rich, new mine of yours to Colonel Edward Hollister."

"Who's this Hollister? He that crooked gambler in Globe?"

"That doesn't concern you. But if it will gain your cooperation, I'll tell you that, no, the colonel is certainly not a gambler, in Globe or anywhere else. He invests only in sure things. Now, what say you just put your mark down here."

"You're crazy, Turner, if you think we're gonna sign that." Anger turned Jason's face deep red.

A smile of satisfaction and anticipation played about Pike Turner's full lips as he slid a pair of thin, black, leather gloves onto his large, knobby knuckled hands. The superior sneer remained as he threw a solid punch into Jason's nose. Blood sprayed to the sides and the sound of breaking cartilage and bone could be heard by everyone. Quickly following it up, Turner smashed heavy blows in under Jason's rib cage, driving the wind from him, hurting and taking pleasure in the hurt.

Stunned and battered beyond endurance, Jason gave a weak cry and fell to the ground, all the defiance driven from him by Turner's furious attack.

"Now, do as I tell you . . . or else."

"Or else what? Are you going to kill us? A lot of good that will do," Bob Gower asserted, trying desperately to find a way out of this. "With us dead, the mine goes to our wives and kids."

Feigning a look of surprise, as though he had forgotten the other prisoners, Turner pivoted half around toward them before answering Bob's challenge. "Ah, yes, the wife and kiddies." With a nod he indicated a short, bow-legged, swarthy man, dressed in striped black trousers, frock coat, vest, and frill-front, white shirt. Although dusty and showing considerable wear, the cuffs slightly frayed, the outfit's expensive quality spoke of the genteel poor.

"LaRoux here is from New Orleans. A Frenchy. He likes to use a knife. Gets downright artistic in what he can do. What say I turn him loose on your wife? He can carve her up any way you'd like."

"You son of a bitch!" Bob Gower surged forward as Turner lashed out once more with his hefty fist. The blow caught Bob in the stomach, staggering him. Turner nodded and two of his men grabbed the miner, holding him tightly.

"No. On second thought, I think I'll let him give you a little demonstration." Turner nodded and LaRoux came forward. A knife appeared suddenly in his hand. It was long and slender, the keen edge glinting in the afternoon sun. Turner reached out and ripped open Bob's shirt and longjohns, exposing the pale, tender flesh of the man's stomach.

LaRoux advanced, the delicate index finger of his left hand brushing daintily at the thin, pencil line of black moustache that adorned his full Gallic upper lip. He wore half-gloves, the flesh of his digits exposed from the second knuckle, and the fingers of his right hand fondled the knife lovingly as he came nearer. His lips moved constantly and, as he approached, Bob could hear through the roar of helpless rage in his mind that LaRoux softly sang the words of a familiar song.

"Frère Jacques . . . Frère Jacques . . . dormez vous?" He stopped before Bob Gower and extended the knife, its tip pressed against the skin of the man's drumtight stomach. *"Allons.* Now we begin, eh?" His voice, lightly accented, had the airy sibilance of a reptile.

Bob Gower shrieked in unbearable pain as the blade entered his flesh, sliding deftly between layers, separating skin from muscle. A trail of molten fire seemed to spread across his abdomen as LaRoux inserted the steel to its full length. The women cried out in horror and drew the children to them, shielding their faces in copious aprons so that they were spared the frightful scene. Bob tried to bite back another scream and failed as LaRoux daintily flicked his wrist, bringing the point of the knife out of his victim's flesh.

Threaded like a needle, now LaRoux applied downward pressure on his slender knife. Bob bellowed in agony and began writhing in the grip of his captors.

"Ça, ça! Do not move so recklessly, *m'sieur.* The work, she make the great mess that way, *non?"* With a practiced twist of his wrist, LaRoux cut free the bottom flap of skin. Reaching out almost fastidiously, he raised the patch of flesh and cut Bob's hide free from his body. LaRoux turned, proudly displaying a seven-inch square of Bob's slightly translucent epidermis. Then in a detached, clinical manner, he bent to inspect his handiwork.

"Bon. Très bon. A bit too much blood, perhaps . . . a small matter, really." Bob Gower trembled violently and, with a pitiful sigh, passed out.

Pike Turner dashed a cup of water into Bob's face, then slapped him violently on one cheek, reviving him. "You ready to sign now, mister?"

"Gaw . . . gu . . . go to hell."

"You may win a place in history as the world's most stubborn fool. You've seen what LaRoux is capable of. How'd you like him to do a little skinnin' job on your wife's tits?"

Gower shrieked in animal fury, struggling with the men who held him. Pike Turner seemed to pay his victim's efforts no mind at all. Smilingly, he went on. "Or, we could turn the ladies over to Nimrod there." Turner's nod directed Bob's blurry gaze toward a huge, hulking Negro who stood guard over the women and children.

As Bob took in the meaning of Turner's words, the black man's pale pink tongue came out to lick thick lips. He grinned in gap-toothed anticipation at his understanding of his boss's suggestion.

"We did a lot of that to you Rebs down in Georgia with Sherman. But, no. I think not just yet." Pike Turner changed his mind. "C.C., you've been nervous as a dog passin' a peach pit ever since we got here. It's a scandal the way you've been eyeing that little cotton-top over there. If you've a mind, what say you go amuse yourself a little?"

A narrow-waisted, slim-hipped young man, one of the pair holding Bob Gower, stepped away, almost simpering in his gratitude at being allowed his own pursuits. He walked cat-footed across the clearing and took Bobby Lee by one arm.

"Leggo me! Leggo, you . . . you . . . " C. C. Steel half-dragged Bobby Lee around behind one of the tents. The little boy's voice continued to yell in protest. "Ow! You're hurtin' me. What are you doin' that for?" Those in front of the tent heard a rending of cloth.

"Ow! Oh, don't . . . don't do *that*! Paw, make him stop! It hurts . . . it hurts . . ." C. C. emitted a forceful grunt and Bobby Lee screamed in pain. He shrieked again, and a third time, then his voice broke into a high, thin wail that faded off into a rhythmic whimper.

"What is he doing? What is he doing to my son?" Clara demanded, her voice quavering.

Pike Turner's reply was bland, detached. "I've no doubt, ma'am, that he's buggerin' him. You see . . . C. C. has some . . . ah, disagreeable traits about him. One of them's his liking for little boys, if you understand the way I mean."

Clara doubled over with pain and grief, her trembling hands covering her face, body wracked with sobs.

40

"Oh, God! Oh, my God. Make him stop. Please, oh, please make him stop."

Bob Gower struggled against the man who held him from behind. "I-I'll sign. Damn you for the bastard you are! I'll sign it. Just make that . . . that animal leave my boy alone."

Pike Turner turned a beaming face on Gower. "I thought you'd see reason eventually. Fine. So much better when gentlemen conduct business in a calm, forthright manner, isn't it? Here. Put your signature on this line . . . and on the copy underneath. That's a good man. Now you."

Al Bartlett, eyes to the ground, shuffled forward under the guns of the others. He extended a trembling hand, took the pen Turner offered and scratched his "X." In the background, Bobby Lee's whimpering grew in volume until he shrieked in pain once more. Turner looked up.

"That's enough for now, C. C. Let the boy go," Turner commanded.

C. C. Steel came around the tent alone, buttoning his trousers. "You're always spoiling everything, Turner," he pouted. "You're nothing but a cruel, insensitive beast."

Turner ignored him, turning to Jason, who lay in a pain-drawn fetal position on the ground. "And now you, mister. You're the last. Just sign here."

Jason averted his eyes from the others while he agonizingly dragged himself to his feet. Shame tasted bitter in his mouth and he raged inwardly at his own impotence. He found himself unable to look his partners in the face.

Jason reached out with one bloodied hand and grasped the pen. Slowly he traced his name on the paper. As he finished, Turner poked the muzzle of his Colt into Jason's ear and blew the man's brains out the other side of his head. Jason staggered sideways and fell in a boneless heap.

While the rest stood in stunned, horrified immobility, Turner swung the revolver in line with Al's chest and shot him twice in the heart. His last two bullets he

41

pumped into Bob Gower's belly, an inch below the skinned patch. Over the screaming, wailing horror and grief of the women and frightened bawling of the two small children, Pike spoke glowingly to his men.

"Colonel Hollister's gonna be mighty proud of our day's work, boys. We just made him owner of a powerful rich strike. Now y'all amuse yourselves as you like. Remember, we leave no survivors and we make it look like Apaches done it."

Chapter Four

Tanaka Tom Fletcher's change in wearing apparel didn't go so far as to separate him from his *katana*. The long-bladed sword, held in place by a narrow, six-inch-wide, plain-colored *obi*, rested in its familiar place at his left side as he leaned against the bar of a saloon in Goodsprings, Nevada. Several men, as was usual, had given him curious, almost disbelieving looks when he first entered. Attention waned, though, when his outward behavior appeared otherwise normal.

He had asked for a glass of beer, showing his money in advance as was the custom. Taking a deep draught, he inquired if the local blacksmith was a competent farrier. His Morgan stallion had thrown a shoe some two miles out of town and he needed a quick repair. Normal enough things so that passing interest returned to a desultory card game, talk of cattle and the hot, dry weather and one old man, who sat in the corner, whittling a rather expertly executed dog from soft pine. Tom sipped his beer and let the heat of the day ooze out of him. Half turned from the bar, he sensed and smelled the presence of the new arrival long before she pressed a large, soft bosom against his back.

"My sakes, but you're a big one. New in town, ain't ya?"

Tom Fletcher turned, trying to repress a smile. Why were pleasure girls in America so forward . . . so pushy? "Yes, ma'am. Just rode in."

"Stayin' long?"

"Only 'til I get my horse tended to. Needs a shoe."

"That's a shame. I'd . . . like to get to know you better." Her rich, blonde hair, done in sausage curls,

43

swayed as she tossed her head to one side. Tom Fletcher took in her narrow waist, large, creamy breasts that mounded delightfully out of a daringly low-cut bodice and the small, pert mouth that smiled easily, if insincerely. Her tiny, button nose and large, intent eyes reminded him of Suiko-san, the first girl he had ever lain with. Tom suddenly found he wanted a woman, needed one badly. He reached out and took the girl's hand.

"Buy a lady a drink?" she asked.

"Let's go to your room," Tom replied hoarsely, his urgent need showing in his voice.

The large eyes grew even bigger, becoming a deep blue. "Say, now. You sure don't waste your time, do you? Okay with me. But it'll cost you."

"Did I ask how much?"

"N-no. Can you pay?"

"If I had to ask how much, I couldn't really afford it, isn't that right? I have gold, I have the need and . . ."

"You've got me. Let's go."

Once upstairs in the room, with the door bolted, Tom removed his *obi* and swords and laid them on a chair beside the bed. Then he began undressing. He smiled at the girl as he undid the buttons of his shirt.

"We didn't even get introduced proper," the girl began, fumbling with the fastenings of her skimpy costume. "I'm Mary . . . but my real name's Jennifer. Jennifer Harding," she rushed on when she caught sight of his muscular, deeply tanned, hairless torso. She felt surprise and confusion that she had revealed her true name. It violated the code of the working girls, a long-established custom to never confide anything to a john. Yet, here she went, jabbering away like a magpie, telling this perfect stranger her real name. Oh, Lord, if Paw ever found out he'd come after her with a horse-whip. Stammering, she tried to take attention away from her slip.

"W-we don't usually get outta our clothes for customers. But with you . . . it's different." She was still babbling, she realized with a jolt. Trembling, too.

"Glad to know you, Jennifer. I'm Tom," Fletcher

contributed as he pulled off his brown, soft leather boots and slid out of his Levis.

Jennifer noticed that Tom wore for underclothes something that looked like a cross between a breech-cloth and a diaper. Then she went weak in the knees as she observed the straining of the cloth as the swelling behind it proclaimed his eagerness. She hurriedly pulled off her feather-trimmed short dress and drew up her silk shift. She felt a growing moistness at the junction of her legs, a rare experience in her profession, as she stepped out of her ruffled bloomers. She threw back the bedcovers and lay down, legs spread widely, invitingly apart. Then she nearly swooned as he divested himself of the last of his garments and his turgid manhood bobbed hugely into view.

Tom crossed to the bed and knelt on it beside the girl. His hand reached out, finding what he sought in the thickly forested triangle between her legs. Jennifer sighed her approval as Tom stretched out full length beside her, intent on his industrious ministrations. His lips closed over one pink-tipped breast, drawing the nipple erect with a rush. With his other hand he caressed the fevered flesh of her taut abdomen. Jennifer's fingers found what they looked for and encircled, stroked, teased.

Unaccustomed to any sort of foreplay in her business, Jennifer found herself enflamed beyond any previous burst of passion. Even that all-important first time hadn't been like this, there in the hayloft of her father's barn, when she thought she'd been in love.

But what did a twelve-year-old know, she had frequent opportunity to remind herself in the years that followed. Luke Owens had come back to water at that same deep and willing well every evening . . . until the branding and tallying were finished and he moved on at the end of summer. Three years later, after Maw died, she went to work in her first dance hall. Ten cents a dance and two dollars for a quick time in a squalid room behind the long wooden structure where rough, uneducated cowboys came on payday to spend their hard-earned dollars.

Six years had gone by since then and she was still in the same business. Although in a better place and at a higher price. Thank God, she'd been able to hold on to her looks. Not a day over sixteen, all the other girls assured her, their voices purring with suppressed jealousy. But now, oh now, all of it seemed worthwhile. No one had ever reached her quite like this. Her whole body trembled with anticipation, her mouth twisted open, and she cried out.

"Now, Tommy! Oh, please, now. Hurry!"

Before responding to the aroused girl's pleas, Tom took time to arrange the pillows beneath her in a uniquely Japanese manner. Then he placed himself between her writhing legs and lowered his body. He entered her with a rush, driving with all his might. Although she shut her mouth tightly, Jennifer could not contain a shrill squeal of delight.

Exercising all his skill and concentration, like the accomplished master he was, Tanaka Tom made their coupling last an infinitely long and delightful time.

An hour later, Tom Fletcher lay with Jennifer's head cradled in the crook of one arm. It had been good. The next time would be even better. Unlike most American women he had experienced, Jennifer showed promise. The thought made his mind wander back to Suiko-san . . .

When his adopted father, Tanaka Nobunara, had told him the time had come to take him to the *go-shan*, the house of prostitution, the young boy had been filled with curiosity and body-tingling anticipation. His excitement had lasted until they entered the low-doored structure and removed their *gehtas*. Father and son were escorted to the bath, where they splashed about in the steaming tub with a number of the establishment's inmates. Massaged, toweled and dressed in fresh kimonos and *tabis*, they were escorted to the main lounge. Much was made over this being Tommy's first visit. Saki was served and the inhabitants discreetly paraded their charms for him.

"Go on, take your pick," Nobunara urged his son.

46

But Tommy had become unsure of himself, sudden shyness suffused his face with a deep crimson blush. All the girls, though young, were older than he. He didn't know how to ask, how to choose the right one, how to do anything. At last, feeling Nobunara's growing impatience, he reluctantly selected Suiko-san. She was only a little older than Tommy. Hesitantly, still overwhelmed by shyness, he let her lead him by the hand down a hallway to a room enclosed by delicate screens.

An hour and a half later, he returned to the main room. He had a wide, confident, silly grin plastered across his face from ear to ear and he walked on legs that felt as weak as two strands of *shirataki* noodles. His superb confidence in his prowess and might of conquest was dashed soon after, however, when, while bragging to his friends he learned that losing one's virtue at the age of thirteen was considered a bit retarded in Japan . . .

With a heavy sigh, Tom Fletcher brought himself back to the present when he felt tender fingers exploring his body. A grin spread on his face, one as silly as that he had worn at thirteen, when he felt Jennifer reach her goal. Maybe he'd introduce her to the little silken cord with its incredible knots?

"Tommy?" Jennifer inquired in a soft, timid voice. "A-are you ready again, Tommy? Uh . . . oh, you are! You really are!"

"He needs a right hind shoe. You might check out the others while you're at it." Tom Fletcher, feeling sated by the exuberance of Jennifer and now anxious to be on his way, gave instructions to the blacksmith.

"Been in this business nigh onto thirty years, man and boy, mister. I never look at just one hoof on an animal." The barrel-bodied, bullet-headed smith bent to his task, checking the Morgan's feet for signs of needed repair, ending with the right hind leg, the one with the missing shoe. "Split the hoof bringing him in all that way after thrown' the shoe. Gonna need a bit of dressin'."

"I figured that. Do whatever is necessary. I want him in first-class condition."

Cocking a quizzical eye at his customer, the blacksmith chose his words carefully. "You really want him in top shape? Too bad we're not close to the ocean. You could walk him in the salt water mornin' and night for a few days. It would strengthen up those hooves and ankles. Gather you've crossed a lot of desert lately. Can't give you such a treatment, but I can provide warm oil baths and damp salt poultices, if you've the time to spend the night."

"You a veterinarian, too?"

In answer to Tom's question, the blacksmith pointed to the sign hung beside the wide double doors. "Jacob Blum, Blacksmith—Horse Doctoring a Specialty—Low Rates," it read. Tom nodded soberly, accepting the diagnosis.

"All right, Mr. Blum, you do what's best. I have a lot more desert to cover before I come to an ocean."

Tom started to leave, then halted abruptly, stepping back inside the smithy to avoid being run down. A six-up team, pulling a mudwagon stagecoach, clattered to a stop outside. Leaning forward, the driver called into the dark interior of the building.

"Hey, Jake! Jake Blum. I need a couple hot rivets in the boot."

Jake came out to examine the problem. His curiosity raised over the unfamiliar expression and the image it called up, Tom went along. At the rear of the coach, a tall leather compartment, held in place by sturdy straps and buckles, hung askew where one of the leather strips had broken. Jake Blum studied it a moment, hemmed and hawed a bit, then returned to his forge. Treading on the protruding tongue of the bellows, he brought the banked charcoal fire to glowing life. From a box he selected four large copper rivets and dropped the male ends onto a pan sitting on the blaze. He selected an awl and returned to the stage.

"It'll be a few minutes, Harv. Why don't you step down and relax. There's coffee on inside."

"Sure thing, Jake. You hear about the Apache raid down Arizona way?"

"No. Didn't know they were off the reservation. What band was it?"

"Nobody said, that I heard. Funny, that. Usually everybody knows just who's on the warpath and who's all cooped up on the reservations."

"Was it bad? I got a distant cousin down that way. Name of Goldwater. He has a mercantile in Tucson."

Harvey grinned encouragement. "Nothin' to worry about on his account then. This happened some ways from there. Up on the Mogollon Rim. That's an odd thing, too. Wasn't any ranches they hit, run off the stock, that sort of thing. Massacreed a bunch of goldminers and their families."

"How many mines were attacked?" Tom Fletcher entered the conversation.

The stage driver started to answer, then stopped, a peculiar expression crossing his face. "By dang, as far as I know . . . only one. But it was 'Paches, sure enough. Tortured 'em, mutilations an' . . . well, they had their way with the women and kids a'fore they finished 'em. Filthy beggars, the lot of them," he spat, swearing darkly.

"Isn't it unusual for the Apaches to strike at only one place?"

"That it is, stranger. Depends, though, on how many of 'em went renegade. Back durin' the war, ol' Mangus Colorado went out with fourteen bucks. They kept the army run ragged for eight months. Must have raided thirty, forty ranches in Arizona an' Mexico. Another time he an' three others left the reservation and hit only one place, didn't even kill the folks there, just ran off ten, twelve head of scrawny cattle, drove 'em back to the *rancheria* and everyone had a big feast. With Apaches you can't always tell."

"Need your help for a minute, if you don't mind, mister," Jake Blum interrrupted the conversation, handing a heavy bucking bar to Tom. He went back to his forge and returned with a smithing hammer and one

49

of the hot rivets in a long pair of tongs. Slipping it into the cold, female half that stuck through the mended leather strap, he showed Tom where to hold and then mashed the copper rivet into place with a stout blow. He repeated this for the remaining three.

"That'll be four bits, Harv."

"Thank you, Jake. I'll be a bit late on the run, but that won't be nothin' new." He paid the blacksmith and mounted to his seat on the stage. Looking down at Tom Fletcher, he added a word of advice.

"If you're headed down Arizona way, mister, I'd keep a close watch on my hair, were I you."

"I'll keep that in mind." The coach rolled away and Tom walked back toward the cafe to take an early supper. His stomach had still not become accustomed to the odors of cooking meat and stale grease, but he realized if he were to prepare his own food, it would raise eyebrows and might lead to an unnecessary confrontation. To his surprise, the cafe, when he entered it, didn't smell of old meals, cooked and forgotten. He took a place at an empty table and, looking up, saw the reason. The kitchen was separated from the main building in the Spanish manner, located outside in a walled enclosure that could be seen through a bead-curtained opening at the rear. A smiling, slightly overweight young woman came to take his order.

"What'll you have?"

Tom selected from the side dishes listed on one half of a hand-printed menu. "I'll have a bowl of beans, some greens, rice, and do you have some tea?"

"Sure do. You want a steak with that?"

Wincing at the suggestion, Tom thought of the American version of beefsteak. Most often tough and stringy, smelling of the rancid grease in which it had been fried to a leather dryness, it didn't at all resemble the tender, succulent Kobi beef which he had enjoyed on infrequent festival days at home in Edo. "No. Do you have any fish?"

"Got some fresh-caught catfish and some mountain trout all iced down."

"I'll take the catfish. And can you, ah, boil it?"

50

The waitress looked at him in consternation, then shrugged. "I suppose so. You're the one's gotta eat it an' you're payin' for it."

While he waited for his food, Tom gave thought to the report of the stage driver. Something about it bothered him. The tale seemed, somehow, to lack rightness, harmony. Think like the *Ainu* boy looking for the lost horse, he admonished himself. If I were a horse, where would I be? Apaches could not eat gold. And, if they were like other tribes he had learned of since returning to his homeland, they didn't use it for money. Only white men sought the yellow metal for its value. Could this be the lead he was looking for? Mutilations by white men? Who then? His mind went back to the description of the massacre of his family, provided him by General Tomlinson. This sounded like the fine, but evil, hand of Edward Hollister might somehow be mixed in. Perhaps, when he reclaimed his horse the next morning he would ride to the Mogollon Rim—wherever that was—and satisfy himself on that score.

Pike Turner sat alone at a table along one side of the largest, most crowded saloon in Globe, Arizona. He and his men had braved the hazards of Salt River gorge and climbed up out of the canyon to Globe. He waited now for the man who employed him. Upon arrival, Turner had telegraphed Edward Hollister at his office in Phoenix. Two hours later, the reply came that Hollister would join them in Globe. Turner poured himself another shot of rye and bided his time.

Half an hour later, an imposing figure, for all his lack of stature, entered imperiously through the batwings. His steel-gray eyes swept the room, located Pike Turner and he started that way. Highly polished boots of rich leather shined even inside the dim saloon and solid silver, rowelless cavalry spurs twinkled in the lamplight. As he approached the table, Edward Hollister pushed back the level brim of his flat-crowned, reddish-brown hat, so that his features became illuminated. He brushed idly at his full, but neatly trimmed, moustache.

"Well, Captain Turner, congratulations on your successful mission." Hollister drew out a chair and unbuttoned his Western-cut, velvet-lapelled, corduroy coat, exposing an expanse of silk vest, with a heavy, gold watchchain spanning its girth. He seated himself as Turner raised his eyebrows in a surprised response.

"*Captain,* is it? Since when?"

"Yes. I thought you deserved a promotion for this most lucrative operation. Besides, you'll soon have an independent command of your own." Hollister affected sleek, close-cropped sideburns in the Latin fashion and his hair was trimmed almost to a dandy's precision, yet he exuded every air of a prosperous, mutton-chopped banker. His full, sensuous lips quirked into a vague smile as he continued to watch Turner's amazed reaction.

"Ah . . . well, now Colonel. What sort of independent command did you have in mind?"

"For some time now, Pike, I have been giving consideration to establishing a special tactical unit. Your inventiveness and aggressive execution of orders recommends you to lead it. I would suggest that the men you currently command be made into a cadre. Despite their many . . . distasteful personal habits, I find them useful. As I am sure you do." Hollister accepted a glass of rye, drank deeply, smacking his lips.

"Always the best, eh, Pike? Now, to what I was saying. From time to time, situations arise that require the particular talents of these . . . ah, gentlemen. A point in fact is our up-coming foray into Mexico. With someone of your proven ability and loyalty in charge. I need not worry about their ambition exceeding their common sense."

"Why, they've been with you as long as I have, Colonel. Surely you can trust them."

"True . . . with a couple of notable exceptions. Nimrod Jackson came to us from that plantation outside Atlanta, remember? And LaRoux. A deserter from the Confederates. If I recall correctly, he was under sentence to hang for the murder of a superior officer. A rather messy killing with a knife, wasn't it? He managed to escape, only to land in our hands."

"They've been faithful ever since."

"Yes, they have. And I have not overlooked that it is you who have kept them so. To other matters, though. I want to record that transfer deed and head back to Phoenix. The city is absolutely full of pigeons waiting to be plucked. I have fond plans of selling that gold mine several times over."

"Why not keep it to help finance the plan, sir?"

"There's too much . . . blood spilled on the claim. It could be that someone might take it in mind at a time in the future to look further into the . . . shall we say, clouded circumstances of my acquiring it. Once it has passed through several hands, nothing untoward can fall back on us. Now for your part.

"You will take your men from here tomorrow. Pick up a detachment of men under Sergeant Dawson at Phoenix and then move out for Ajo. You know what to do when you get there.

"So, if you're ready, let's be on our way."

Chapter Five

Growling over the rock-strewn, desert land, a rolling sound like thunder reached Tanaka Tom Fletcher's ears. He reined up sharply, listening carefully.

There. Again. This time the rumbling separated itself into individual sounds, making up a ragged volley. Shots were being exchanged somewhere not far ahead. Tom Fletcher eased himself in the saddle and leaned slightly forward, giving the dark, roan Morgan a light tap with the heels of his soft, brown boots. Obediently the animal started out at a cautious, quick-footed pace. As Tom drew near to a gap between two sandy, cactus-covered hills, the firing reached a pitch, then dwindled off. Tom nosed his horse to the right, off the trail, and made his way to a spot near the top of the mound. Dismounting, he crawled to the crest and looked onto the trail below.

In the distance, he saw a stagecoach, stopped in the middle of the road. Beside it lay the stretched out body of a man. From inside the coach came the shrill, frightened cries of two small children. Half a dozen men busied themselves around the outside of the mudwagon.

Two of the scruffy-looking crew worked to unhitch the team, separating two horses to serve as pack animals. On top of the rig, a thick-waisted individual dumped the body of the guard off onto the sand. At the back of the coach, two men went industriously through the contents of the luggage boot. From his *obi*, Tanaka Tom drew his Dollond. The compact, pocket-size telescope brought the figures into close relief.

The men were unshaven, their clothes faded and worn, showing signs of much patching. After a cursory examination of each of them, Tom concentrated his attention on the pair at the rear of the mudwagon. At the back of the boot, buried under the articles belonging to the passengers, they found what they sought. Straining under the weight, they lifted out a large, heavy strongbox and sat it on the ground. The taller of them drew his revolver and blew off the lock. He threw back the lid and three others hurried to gather around.

At the sound of the shot, a thin wail came from inside the coach and a childish voice begged for mercy. The muscles of Tom Fletcher's jaw hardened and his mouth drew into a grim line. If his thoughts were right about Hollister being somehow involved with the murder of those miners, then his men should still be somewhere around this part of Arizona. The method used in this stage holdup, with all the witnesses being killed, saving the children for last, fitted the style of Hollister's sadistic degenerates. That being the case, he needn't look further. His decision made, Tom left his position and moved rapidly to his ground-tied animals. He hobbled the mule and took from one pack his *katana*, leaving the scabbard behind. Swinging into the saddle, he urged his Morgan around the far side of the hill. He wanted to come upon the site of the holdup with the sun at his back.

When he reached the position he wanted, Tom thought over what he might use as a diversion, something to let him get within killing range before the advantage of the enemies' firearms could cancel his element of surprise. His mind rapidly considered and discarded several things. Then he came up with the one factor that united the honest man and the outlaw for mutual protection. Dropping his *katana* low along the side of his horse, out of sight of anyone in front of him, he drummed his heels into the Morgan's ribs. The stout-chested animal leaped forward into a full gallop and thundered down toward the stage.

Tanaka Tom opened his mouth wide, shouting, "Indians! Indians!"

* * *

"There she is, boys," Bart Colton proudly exclaimed, exposing the tightly packed ranks of double eagles to the avaricious eyes of his gang. "Just like that drunk little army clerk told us. Fresh minted in San Francisco and on the way to Fort Apache. Imagine sendin' money to *buy* Apache land."

"Reckon we ought to be grateful they didn't send along a cavalry escort, eh, Bart?"

"Right enough, Phil." Inside the coach, a child wailed in protest while another sobbed softly.

"Please don't hurt us, mister, please."

"What we gonna do with them?"

Bart Colton leered wickedly. "We can't leave 'em around to describe us, Eb. Especially with you ridin' on the coach as inside man. Make it quick and as painless as you can. Of course, one of them brats is a girl . . . and right close to bein' ripe for the pickin' at that."

Eb made a face. "They ain't to my likin' that young, Bart."

"If they're old enough to bleed, they're old enough to butcher," Bart growled through a leer.

Eb turned to obey his leader's order when the outlaws heard the sounds of pounding hoofs. They looked up and saw a lone rider bearing down on them. Phil threw his Henry rifle to his shoulder. Then they heard the high, clear voice, shouting a single word over and over, one that sent a chill along their spines, despite their hardened, cruel natures.

"Indians! Indians!"

Phil lowered his weapon and exchanged a nervous glance with Bart Colton. "Now that really ties it," the gang leader exploded, bending to take one handle of the strongbox. Another man stooped to help him and they hurried toward the pack-rigged coach horses. Phil stood where he was, waiting for the man to come up to him.

At a full gallop, the stranger plunged forward, until only a few feet from the standing outlaw. Then he reined sharply to the left, his mount's hoofs throwing out a spray of sand. Through the cloud of dust and grit, Phil saw what looked like a bright shaft of light springing from the rider's hand as he lifted his arm high in the air. Phil didn't hear the thin swishing sound, but he felt a numbing, fire-and-ice pain rush through his body as Tanaka Tom Fletcher's *katana* cleaved neatly through him from collarbone to navel. The bisected outlaw dropped his rifle and fell away in two directions as blackness overtook his mind.

Looking back over his shoulder, Bart Colton witnessed the destruction of Phil Nichols. He dropped his end of the strongbox and hastily drew his revolver. He threw a round in the direction of the mounted man with the sword. The fat .44 slug whistled through empty air. Cursing, Bart eared back the hammer for a second try as Red O'Donnel, on top of the coach, blasted away with his Spencer.

Tanaka Tom felt himself being lifted from the saddle before he experienced pain from the grazing bullet. The heavy .52 caliber slug burned along his ribs, parting skin and muscle, but not penetrating his chest cavity. He fell heavily, beside Phil's body, and his Morgan, combat wise from Tom's patient training, jumped into the clear. For a moment, Fletcher lay stunned, the wind knocked from his body. When he failed to return their fire, the outlaws took heart and charged his position.

Reaching out quickly, Tanaka Tom retrieved the dead outlaw's Henry rifle and, checking to see if a round was in the chamber, aimed at the nearest holdup man. Unaccustomed to firearms, he jerked the trigger. The bullet went low, striking Eb in the groin.

The big man screamed shrilly and his legs lost their ability to hold him up. He tumbled forward, somersaulting head over heels to lie on his back, a bright pool of blood spreading between his legs. Tom worked the unfamiliar lever and chambered another rim-fire shell. Not even trying to sight properly, he quickly blazed off three more shots and the outlaws dived for cover. Red O'Donnel, on top of the stage, rose to his knees and took careful aim. As his finger eased up slack, Tanaka Tom rolled to the right, one hand going to his *obi*.

Tom's hand came out with a *shuriken*. He drew back

57

his right arm and made a straight, power throw, sending the small death star twinkling through the air. It struck O'Donnel in the stomach, just below the diaphragm. Dropping his rifle he clawed at the burning poison that surged into his vitals from the painful points buried in his flesh. As his head went back, Tom threw a second *shuriken*, this one ending its flight with one point buried in O'Donnel's neck, severing a carotid artery.

O'Donnel convulsed heavily, dislodging the five-pointed death star from his throat. Blood fountained out after it and the outlaw slumped feebly to a sitting position. He held his pose until his frantically pumping heart caused him to leak to death. Tanaka Tom didn't wait to watch the death drama.

In the same instant he completed his second throw, he snatched up his *katana*, with the rifle in his other hand, and dashed around to the off-side of the coach. Now he had the mudwagon between him and the other gunmen. He waited tensely, but they made no further moves. Inside the stage, the children screamed hysterically. Tanaka Tom started toward the front of the conveyance, then abruptly reversed direction and hurried around the back, the way he had come.

Finger curled around the trigger of the Henry, he shoved the muzzle of the rifle forcefully under a surprised Bart Colton's chin. The keen edge of the *katana* hovered a scant few inches from the exposed throat of another man. The third robber, behind them and with no clear field of fire, surrendered to the obvious, threw down his revolver and raised his hands.

"You got us, mister. I give up," he sighed out laconically.

"Yellow-belly bastid," Bart Colton growled. Then, realizing his own death waited only a split second away, he relaxed his grip on his sidearm and let the Remington thud to the sand. "Looks like he's got us, Bill," he told the man beside him.

In a few minutes Tom had them securely bound. At gunpoint he made Bart tie up his two men, then Tom lashed Colton tightly and inspected the knots on the others. Satisfied, he strode to the coach and opened the door.

A cooling corpse fell out almost into his arms, and he saw another blood-spattered body slumped in the far corner. Turning his head to the left his eyes took in an ashen-faced little girl recoiling violently into the cushion, a small hand covering her shrieking mouth. Beside her, a trembling boy about two years younger stared at Tom big-eyed and silently wet his trousers.

"Here, now. I'm not going to hurt you. The bad men who stopped your stage are . . . taken care of. It's all right now." He reached out a firm, big hand. "Come on, little girl, it's all over."

"D-daddy. T-they k-ki-killed my daddy," the girl sobbed. Tears ran down the boy's face, too. His carrot-top identified him as her brother. Tom was struck again by the difference between American and Japanese children. He would have to make an effort to spare them further anguish.

"Let's get out of the coach," Tom urged. "Don't look at the bodies."

He led the youngsters away from the scene of bloody violence, to a spot among the rocks where a thin spring kept a pair of cottonwood trees alive. Taking a handkerchief from his pocket he bathed both their faces and encouraged them to take a drink. When the gulping and sobbing subsided, Tanaka Tom asked the question foremost in his mind.

"The man with the sword . . . the sabre? . . . did he leave before I got here?"

The girl regarded Tom for several moments in solemn, big-eyed silence. Then she gulped back another sob of grief and horror, licked her lips and made a reply.

"No. There was no one like that here."

Chapter Six

Samurai training prevented Tom Fletcher's disappointment from showing on his face. So Hollister had not himself been involved in this. Perhaps the surviving outlaws could provide him better information. He walked to where they lay and rolled Bart Colton onto his back with the toe of his boot.

"What is your name?"

"Go to hell."

Tom brought the heel of one boot down sharply, an inch below Colton's diaphragm. "I can do this the easy way or the hard way. The choice is yours."

After the outlaw recovered from the dizzying blackness that overwhelmed him when Tom's *kasoku-tei* kick drove the wind from his lungs, he replied weakly. "Colton . . . Bart Colton."

"That's better. Who do you work for?"

"Who? . . . I, uh, we don't work for anybody. I'm the boss."

"You ever heard of Edward Hollister? Colonel Edward Hollister?"

A light glinted in Colton's eyes. "Sure. Who hasn't?"

"But you do not work for him?"

"I wish I did. He's big, mister. You got any quarrel with him, you'd best forget all about it. Word is he owns governors, judges, congressmen. Nobody gets close to him. Not even fellers on the owlhoot. I know. I tried, but he don't take on anyone. He's got enough men, the way it was told me, to do what he wants."

"And what is that?"

Colton grunted a short, bitter laugh. "Think Hollister confides in one like me? Hell, I didn't even see him. I

60

talked to a feller named Turner. Pike Turner. 'The colonel regrets, but we are taking no new recruits,' he says. Like they was runnin' some damned army."

Tanaka Tom silently considered this information for a few seconds. Pike Turner's name was on the general's list, right enough, along with so many others. This Colton . . . shabbily dressed as the men he claimed to lead. All considered, he no doubt told the truth. When Tom spoke again, he changed the subject.

"There are a lot of dead men here."

"Leave 'em for the buzzards."

"No. You and your companions are going to bury them."

"What? Like hell we are."

Tom lowered the keen edge of his *katana* until it rested a few inches above Colton's exposed throat. "You will bury them . . . or join them."

"All right, all right! Sure, mister, whatever you say."

That solved one problem. Smiling, Tom Fletcher turned to the children. "What is your name, little girl?"

"A-Amy." She wiped at one reddened eye with a small fist. Then, as though reciting something learned by rote, she went on. "This is my brother, Peter. He's nine. We live in Payson. Our last name is Carson. The-these men killed our daddy."

"I know. How far is Payson, Amy?"

"Oh . . . maybe twenty, thirty miles. I don't know."

"But you do know which way?"

"Oh, sure. Over there." She pointed in the direction the stage had been heading when stopped by the robbers.

"Fine. Now we are going to have to . . . do something for those who died. Can you and Peter look out for yourselves while we do that?" The girl solemnly nodded. "Good."

Tanaka Tom untied the three remaining outlaws and set them to work digging graves, under the threatening muzzle of a six-gun he had taken from one of them. Time passed slowly as the sun climbed to the zenith and began lowering in the sky. On the western horizon a few puffy balls of cloud gathered, grew, darkened, though still looking far away. In two hours time seven shallow graves had been completed.

After the bodies had been placed in the holes and covered over with sand and ample rocks to discourage roving predators, the survivors gathered around the mounds. Amy and Peter were crying quietly now, eyes cast downward on their father's resting place. The outlaws shuffled their feet, feeling uncomfortable. Tanaka Tom looked over the oddly assorted group, his mind on the immediate future. He couldn't leave the children here . . . or let them strike out for home alone. That meant they would all travel together. In the long silence, he noticed that all eyes had turned toward him. He cleared his throat.

"If it is your custom, I suppose you will want to say something over the graves of your companions."

Bart Colton looked surprised. "You mean me, mister? Hell, I wouldn't know where to start."

"So be it." He glanced at Amy.

The girl began a brief, childish prayer, breaking into sobs part way through. With Peter's help, she finished. Once more, everyone seemed to be waiting for Tom to make the decisions.

"Our battle seems to have run off all but two of your horses," he observed laconically. "A shame. That limits our water supply, as well as making a difficult journey. Can you ride a horse?" he directed the question to Peter.

"Sure!" The boy brightened. "You bet, mister."

"Good. Go and make the stirrups the right size for you and your sister." His grief forgotten in his sudden self-importance, the boy scampered away.

"What are we gonna ride?" Bart Colton asked in a tone of protest.

"You'll have to make do with the coach horses. Come."

Near the stage animals, Tom had Colton tie the others face down on the ground. Then the young samurai ordered the outlaw leader onto one broad-backed mount. Bending, his eyes and gun muzzle not leaving

Colton's back, he tied the stage robber's ankles together under the belly of the horse. Then, the sharp point of his *ho-tachi,* the short sword, against Bart's side, he secured the man's hands.

One by one, he repeated his actions for the others. Next he attached a lead rope from the halter of one animal to the other. He extended a longer piece to where the children were waiting beside the outlaws' horses.

"Peter, tie this to the saddle horn. You and Amy will ride ahead of them and I'll be behind. It will be up to you to set the pace. Keep the line tight. If they try to ride you down, I'll shoot them. But the prime responsibility is yours. Think you can do it?"

"Yes, sir!" the boy squeaked.

"Good boy. Let's ride."

Tanaka Tom swung into the saddle of his Morgan and took his place behind the outlaws. Amy rode out first, her little brother following. Peter drummed his heels into the skittish roan's ribs until he felt the rope draw tight. Looking back, a grin of confidence on his face, he waved to Tom. The samurai fell into line, leading his recovered pack mule, and the small caravan loped down the road.

Behind them, in the far distance, a muted growl of thunder rolled across the desert hills. A sudden, stout, chill wind sprang up, scattering stinging bits of sand ahead of it. Unseen by the eastward-bound riders, a dust cloud rose, hovering ominously behind them.

Two hours later, the dust billowed around them. The wind increased to gale force. Sharp-edged grains of sand bit into the riders' faces, and visibility waned rapidly. Tanaka Tom could barely see the slender form of the small boy who led the string of trussed outlaws. Above them the sky blackened more, not with clouds, but with tons of wind-borne dust and grit. Tom's Morgan stallion trembled and snorted nervously, trying to clear his caked nostrils. Tom galloped forward, ordering a halt in the dubious shelter of a high pile of rocks.

"We have to find a place to wait out this storm," Tom shouted above the constant scream of wind.

Bart Colton had grown pale, a greenish tinge about his features. "We can't go on! We'll be lost . . . wander out here for days."

"We can still see the road," Tom countered. "As long as we follow that, we'll be all right. But the horses can't take much more of this."

"We'll be lost, I tell you! We'll all die!"

Sensing the man's near-hysteria, Tanaka Tom lashed out with an open hand, slapping Colton's cheek with enough force that the outlaw nearly fell from his saddleless mount. "You need a drink. Give them all some water," he commanded Peter, lifting his canteen. Tom dismounted and went to his pack mule. He located some strips of cloth and wet them from one of the robber's water bottles. Giving Amy instructions, both of them began to gently bathe the frightened animals' muzzles, at last tying the damp cloths over their flaring nostrils.

"Let's go," Tom ordered. "Keep your eyes down, on the road, let your horse pick his own way," he commanded the children. Masking their own faces with damp bandanas, the riders moved out.

Olney Mathers decided he'd had enough. Going on could only lead to a gallows' rope and their chances of surviving the storm, if they kept moving, were nil. Either way, he had no desire to die. Visibility had been so reduced now that he could not see the horses carrying Bart and Lew ahead of him. Nor, he assured himself by turning to peer over his shoulder, could he see that madman with the sword. Bending far forward over his mount's withers, he fumbled with numb, bound hands, fingers struggling to untie the lead rope.

Kneeing the animal forward a little gave Olney some slack. Working patiently, he felt the first knot give and a sweep of elation flooded his body. With the infinite patience of a condemned man, he tugged and wrestled with the final bend in the line.

After several false starts, it yielded and he watched

the lead string drop free, disappearing in the distance as he urged his horse to turn to one side. Carefully he counted the paces, halting after ten, and listening to the soft plop of Tom Fletcher's Morgan and the grunting protests of the pack mule as they passed by, unaware, in the distance.

Olney breathed a sigh of relief as the hoofbeats cut off, swallowed by the storm. He rested a moment, then turned his mount and headed back ten carefully counted paces to the trail. A short struggle freed his hands and he bent to untie his feet. A wind-driven clump of sagebrush bounded over the ground, lifting occasionally to sail through the air, masked from view by the thick swirl of sand and dust. As Olney leaned far out, precariously unbalanced, the spiny bush struck his horse's rump.

"Hey, mister! Hey!" Amy trotted back to where Tom Fletcher kept the rear guard. Her voice was muffled by the sand-encrusted bandana around her nose and mouth. "There's a place up ahead. Only a little bit of a way."

"Good girl. Sure you can find it again?"

Amy thrust out an unseen pink lower lip in a pout. "Of course I can."

"Then lead the way."

Gradually, out of the darkness, a deep, bowl-like depression in the ground began to take form as Tom and the others rode forward. High rocky sides buffered the worse effects of the storm, and a shallow pool, surrounded by stunted trees, offered even more protection. Tom swung tiredly from the saddle, feeling the effort of fighting the raging storm. His eyes scanned the sky, grunting with satisfaction as he saw that the worst effects of the whirling, biting sand were being carried far above them. As he turned around, Peter came rushing to him, his big, blue eyes wide with worry and fear.

"Where's the other one, mister?"

"Other what, Peter?"

"There's only two of them owlhoots here. One of them got away. He'll kill us for sure!"

Chapter Seven

The coach horse Olney Mathers had escaped on struggled on hopelessly broken legs. Its flanks heaved with the effort to breathe, as it tried to stand.

Each time, it fell back with pitiful cries, strangely like those of a small child in great pain. The odd, unbalanced burden that had clung to it during the flight through the dust storm—now flopping on the ground, now tangled between the steed's hind legs—still hampered its movements. Fear departed with the diminished winds and return of visibility. As panic lessened, like something dimly remembered, the animal recalled the soothing voice and gentling hands of man. The roan whinned softly and it ceased its struggles as it calmed and waited for help to come.

"Looks like that's the last of it," Tanaka Tom Fletcher observed, lips and tongue working to expel grit from his mouth."

"None too soon, either. Don't know if we could have held these horses much longer."

Tom raised a quizzical eyebrow. He found Bart Colton's change in attittude, brought on by the storm, a strange contrast to the man's past. All the same, he determined not to relax his vigilance. He led his Morgan to the pool, washed sand from the animal's nostrils, and let it drink. Around him the others were doing the same.

"I'm going back to look for your partner. You will be bound again. Do not try to escape."

Colton shrugged expansively, as if flight was the farthest thing from his mind. "We're caught now an' that's the truth of it. Just have to take our chances with the judge. Appreciate you goin' back after Olney. They's some as would leave him out there to die."

Tanaka Tom pulled his lips into a thin line, approximating a smile. "My motives aren't humanitarian. Like Peter said when he first noticed the escape, Olney could kill us all. I don't want a man out there trailing us."

Bart Colton turned away with a strangled curse. Then he pitched face-first into the sand, shoved violently from behind by Tanaka Tom, who quickly tied him up. Tom repeated his efforts with the other outlaw and turned to the children.

"You know how to use this?" he asked Peter, handing the boy a Colt 1872 revolver.

"Sure I do."

"What about me, mister? I can use a gun. An' I'm older."

Tom looked up at Amy, surprise on his face. A girl? He'd never considered the possibility. Hmmm. But, why not? In the old days, samurai women often fought beside their men, some of them, as the old tales said, even more viciously than their male counterparts. He reached into one pack on his mule, where he had stored the accumulated weapons of the outlaws, withdrawing another revolver.

"All right, Amy. If one of them tries to escape, kill both." Tom swung into the saddle and started out along their backtrail.

An hour's fruitless search brought the day almost to ending. The wind's howling fury had blotted out any sign of a trail, smoothing the desert's surface to a uniform sameness, as though life itself had yet to emerge in this barren land. Tom decided on one more zig-zag sweep, taking him even further from their oasis camp, when he heard the distant, plaintive whinny of a horse. He set heels to the Morgan and headed in that direction.

Using the cries as a guide, Tom Fletcher soon located what was left of Olney Mathers. His feet still tied, the man had somehow lost his balance and fallen, to be dragged by the frightened horse until it had fallen over the side of a low wash, breaking both forelegs. Nothing could be done for the animal or its rider, so Tom drew his *katana* and quickly put the critter out of its misery. Then he turned his attention to Olney Mathers.

Little remained of the man except bone, gristle, and blood-soaked clothes. Tom first thought of burying the man where he lay. Then he recalled the suspicious nature of all men in authority. After his experience in Washout, he decided he'd better have all the proof he could collect for the law. Removing his mackintosh from the leather ladigo straps, he knelt beside the corpse. Tom rolled the battered body into his rubberized coat and tied the bundle on behind his saddle. Mounting, he rode out toward the oasis.

The night passed uneventfully and everyone prepared to leave early in the morning. While they rode along, Tom thought back to when he had returned to the oasis with Olney Mathers's corpse.

He said nothing about it to the others, but set about preparing food from his small supply. Tom fixed rice and tea and, from dried vegetables, reconstituted in water and dipped in a rice flour batter, *tenpura no-tomo*. Because of the meager size of his larder, he and the children ate well, but the outlaws had to make do with a bowl of rice and, to them, bitter tasting tea. Tanaka Tom sat awake most of the night, keeping guard. He nodded off into a light sleep in the early hours of morning, only vaguely aware of the girl, Amy, taking his place, a heavy Remington revolver cradled in her small lap. Over breakfast, he had gravely thanked her in the solemn way of a samurai, then went to tend the horses they now rode.

"Are you sure of the distance?" Tom asked Amy during their noon halt.

"Much as I can be, mister. I've never ridden by stage before."

"Call me Tom." He took another short swallow from the canteen and passed it around. A few minutes later he signaled for them to mount.

Time and distance must be measured on a different scale for a child, Tom considered when evening found them still some unknown distance from Payson, Arizona. Reluctant to halt, although he acknowledged the need for the youngsters if not for himself, Tom sought a place to stop for the night. As preparations went forward for the evening meal, the two outlaws talked quietly among themselves.

"By God, we gotta get away from here. Them people in Payson'll hang us for sure."

"Not so loud, Lew, you ninny," Bart Colton growled. "Way I figure it, we'll make Payson before noon tomorrow. You're right about the reception we'll get. So I've been working on it. That's why I been butterin' him up. Get him to drop his guard. Later tonight we'll do something about this. I managed to steal a knife from the cookin' stuff."

Darkness fell swiftly across the desert. Rolled in blankets, to ward off the night's chill, everyone settled down to sleep. Amy had volunteered to stand the first watch and, smiling at the girl's courage and determination, Tanaka Tom had allowed her to do so, with a brief admonition.

"Keep a good eye on those two. When the moon's high up overhead, wake me."

"Yes, sir . . . ah, Tom."

Despite the excitement of their adventure, a long, hard day's ride in the saddle soon put Amy into head-nodding slumber. Bart and Lew, who had listened to the rustling preparations for night, raised their heads cautiously to gauge their chances. A small, motionless mound revealed Peter's position and a larger one showed where Tom Fletcher slept until his turn at guard. Satisfied, Bart Colton produced the knife and cut himself and his partner free. Crouching low, massaging numbed wrists, Lew leaned close to Bart's head, whispering directly into his ear.

"We gonna take all the horses and clear out?"

"Just that good lookin' Morgan and our own *caballos*, Lew. We ain't leavin' no witnesses, so the rest of the stock can fend for themselves."

69

Lew seemed to hesitate a moment. "I don't know about that, Bart. About the killin', I mean. I can see gettin' that feller with the sword. He's a killer, right enough, and he'd come after us for sure if'n we didn't. But the others . . . hell, they're just tads. Don't seem right somehow."

"You were ready enough back at the stage."

"But we didn't know them then. Doin' in strangers is one thing. Now . . ."

"You want to swing for this?" Bart took Lew's silence as capitulation. "Then we do it my way. Come on."

Bart had removed his boots and now started across the sand without the slightest noise. Lew had done the same and he sucked in his breath as they stopped, poised over the silent, motionless form of Tanaka Tom. Bart raised the knife, its slender blade gleaming in the moonlight, and plunged it deeply into the huddled form.

Not a sound escaped the victim. No death throes caused the body to thrash its life away either. Suspicious, fearing the consequences of his sudden thought, Bart swung back the cover. The "dead man" consisted of a bundle of clothes, saddle blankets and the mule's pack-saddle. They had been tricked. Filled with dread and confusion, Bart stood upright, looking widly around.

Only a slight, musical whistling revealed the arrow's path before it struck home.

Tanaka Tom Fletcher had gone through the motions of preparing for sleep, watching carefully to see the two outlaws bedded down and adding fuel to the stack beside the low fire. He positioned Amy on guard and faded into the darkness. From there he had watched Amy nod off into deep sleep and quickly prepared his bedroll to simulate a slumbering form. Taking his *kyujutsu* bow and four *nakazashi* war arrows from the *ebita* quiver made of lacquered wood, leather, and paper, he moved soundlessly in *tabi* slippers to a position overlooking the camp. There he waited.

Near midnight, when the girl had slumped back

70

against the dubious comfort of a sun-heated rock that still gave forth its warmth, he noticed furtive movement under the scraggy cottonwood where he had tied Bart Colton and Lew. Aided by deep breathing and the mental concentration of his *ki* powers, his night sight let him closely observe their efforts. His keen hearing picked out the sound of thin cord parting under a knife's edge and, a few moments later, Tom watched the two outlaws scuttle soundlessly across the campsite to where they believed him to be sleeping.

Nocking an arrow, he held it to the string beside his right eye. Extending his left arm upward to full length, as he had been taught to do by the aged Zen Buddhist priest who had been his archery instructor, then rotating the bow through its own axis until his eye sighted along the shaft, over the ugly, jagged warhead of a "bowel raker" arrow, toward his target. Tom held it thus as Colton bent over, and the slender knife, that the young samurai had seen him pilfer from among the supper dishes, flashed in the air. Tom gave a soft grunt of satisfaction that he had read the man's intentions correctly.

Tom heard the startled gasp when the outlaws discovered his ruse and, as Bart Colton jerked upward, he released the arrow. The superbly made shaft, with its unique *Fujika rentai* ideograph characters on the fletchings, sped true to its target. Bart Colton shrieked with agony and clutched desperately at the feathered shaft as it buried itself in his flesh. Even before the first arrow struck home, a second one flashed through the air.

It pinioned Bart's left hand to his chest, slid between two ribs and pierced his heart. The screaming died in his throat and he pitched onto the ground, stone dead. Beside him, Lew bolted, his eyes wide and goggling white with terror. The third shaft passed through the space vacated by his body. As he ran, the fourth arrow Tanaka Tom fired smacked meatily into his left buttock. Lew tumbled in an awkward somersault, sprawling on the sand, half rising, his arms over his head in surrender.

"Don't, mister. Don't kill me. I give up."

71

Startled awake by Colton's dying screams, Amy bounded upright, her finger twitching on the trigger of the Remington. The big gun went off with a shatteringly loud report, the bullet plowing into the sand a few feet from the wounded man. Shrieking in fright, Lew tried to scuttle sideways across the ground. Tanaka Tom rose from his position in the rocks and stalked toward the terrified man, moonlight glinting off the blade of his *katana*.

"It's all right, Amy. He's not going anywhere."

Lew's eyes fixed on Tanaka Tom's sword, growing wide and losing focus in his horror. "Oh, please, mister. Don't slice me up with that thing. Please!"

Tanaka Tom's lips curled in contempt at a man who would surrender so easily and who would act so cravenly at the sight of a *katana*, which promised, at the least, honorable death. He knelt at the trembling outlaw's side, sheathing the long blade and drawing his small *tano* knife, which was made in the same manner and shape as his *katana*.

"Keep him covered," he instructed Amy over one shoulder. Then Tom slashed deeply into the flesh of Lew's buttock, removing the fore- and backward-curved arrow point that defied any other means of removal. Lew screamed in pain at the incision and again as the blood-and-tissue decorated bowel raker tip came free of his flesh. Trembling with renewed violence, his eyes rolled up in his head and he passed out.

Tanaka Tom took a small kit from his belongings and packed the wound with a poultice of salt and a certain tree fungus that grew in the forests above the sacred temple city of Nara. He bandaged Lew and tied him to the cottonwood. Tom brewed tea and shared it with the children, calming their excitement. In half an hour the entire camp slept.

Three hours after sunrise, they reached their goal. The horses walked soft-footed down the dusty main street of Payson, Arizona, their motley passengers drawing a growing crowd of curious onlookers. Small boys, their bare feet raising puffs of reddish dust, strutted behind, capering and shouting to one another as they recognized Amy and Peter and the corpse of Bart Colton. By the time they reached the sheriff's office, the entire populace of Payson had turned out. Tanaka Tom swung from the saddle and stepped onto the boardwalk. Bowing slightly he addressed the lawman.

"*Ohayō gezaimasu* . . . Good morning . . . Sheriff. These children, Amy and Peter Carson, are from your community, they tell me. Their father was killed in a stage holdup. I have brought in three of the bandits. One of them, as you see, is alive."

Before the startled peace officer could make reply, Lew cried out in panic, appealing to the people of Payson. "Jesus, Mary, and Joseph! Have mercy on me. He killed 'em with a sword . . . cut 'em to pieces. He's a crazy man. Shot Bart with an arrow . . . me too . . . like a stinkin' Injun. He's a mad dog, I say!"

Angry murmurs rose among the denizens of Payson's several saloons, who were scattered among the crowd. Before their bursts of indignation could rise to the danger point, the sheriff spoke.

"That Bart Colton's wild bunch?"

"Yes, sheriff."

"Good riddance to 'em, I say. Come on inside, Mr. . . . ah . . ."

"Fletcher. Tom Fletcher."

"Good enough. Leroy," he addressed a gangling, pock-faced teenager lounging against the wall of the jail. "Go fetch Grandmaw Carson. Don't give her the sad news, but bring her here. Now, step on in, Mr. Fletcher, we have a bit of business to transact."

Once the center of attraction had been removed, the crowd began to disperse. Tom Fletcher relaxed into a straight-back chair placed in front of the sheriff's desk. Tom's eyes took in the scrubbed-clean appearance of the room and of the stout, stern-faced man sitting opposite him, who drew to himself pen, inkwell, and paper, scribbling as he spoke.

"The Butterfield Stage Company has authorized me to pay a reward of one hundred dollars, dead or alive, for Bart Colton and fifty each for the men who rode with him. That makes a total of two-hundred-fifty dollars to you, Mr. Fletcher." The sheriff looked up, a small smile playing on his lips. "Just take this over to the bank and they'll give you gold for it."

"I don't understand. I'm being paid for killing these men?"

"You're getting a reward for bringing them in. Too bad you didn't bring the others. That'd been another hundred and fifty. Though I will say that killin' 'em did save the cost of a trial."

"All the same, I thank you." Tanaka Tom started to rise. "Now, if there is nothing more, I will be on my way."

"You're free to go, Mr. Fletcher, with my thanks for a job well done. Is there . . . something else?"

Tanaka Tom turned back before reaching the door. "Do you know of an Edward Hollister? Colonel Hollister?"

The sheriff gave it some thought. "No. A new one on me. He wanted for something?"

"He is wanted by me, yes. Well then, I'll take my leave now. Thank you."

Outside, as Tom led his Morgan to the livery stable, he examined the note. A strange custom, he thought, but one he would keep in mind for the future.

Chapter Eight

In the dry creekbed, a small fire burned that only partially kept back the deep chill of the desert night. The men of the small detachment now commanded by Pike Turner lounged back against the high bank sheltering them from the sharp wind that blew lightly from the south. They listened closely as Turner described their tactics for looting the small village of Ajo, Arizona, a half-day's ride from where they camped. When he finished, one man spat a long stream of tobacco juice and shifted uncomfortably.

"What I cain't see is why we don't just ride in hell-for-leather, grab off ever'thing worth takin' and get the devil out."

"Because we have our orders. This is the way the colonel wants it done. We gotta hold the town for two days. Colonel Hollister will be meetin' us there." More than a week had passed since Pike Turner's conversation with Colonel Hollister. They had covered a lot of ground and had nothing to show for it. Pike realized the men needed some encouragement, something to keep them sharp. Casting aside his orders to the contrary, he decided to reveal a bit of the larger plan to his troops.

"There's something big fixin' to happen down Mexico way. The colonel, he figures to be there when it does, so's to pick off the biggest piece of the pie for himself. You boys have been chosen to share in part of that. Now," he turned to a crouched, uneasy, nervous-looking man near him by the fire. "Let's hear what it is you think's so important Colonel Hollister knows of it."

Joe Coaker raised the bandaged stubs of his fingers

so that the firelight glowed red-yellow on them. "Here. See these. Boys, I tell you, you've never seen the like. This feller came swaggerin' into the saloon there in Washout like he owned the whole world and ever'thing in it. Frank an' me was funnin' him a bit when all of a sudden-like he whips out this big ol' sword and does Frank in. I mean to say, fellers, he moved that blade around so fast it was nothin' but a bright blur. 'Fore I knowed it, he up and cut off Frank's gunhand . . . and his head . . . and he done this to me. That's why we didn't do that bank job in Washout. I got to thinkin' the colonel should hear about it direct, so's not to think we let him down, or tried to keep the loot for ourselves. Worst part, the sheriff let the feller go. Said a knife again' a gun was more than a fair fight."

"That's all?" Pike Turner felt a slight disappointment in the rambling unimportance of the tale brought by this small-time hardcase who came to babble excuses instead of deliver as promised.

"That . . . an' . . . well, it seemed sorta funny at the time. Almost like this feller dressed odd-like to get someone to call him out. More'n that, sorta as if he was after Frank, direct. What I mean, a'fore the fight began he up and and introduced himself. Said his name used to be Tommy Frecher back before he got to be called . . . ah, Takka . . . Tommo . . . ah, some mouthful of damn rice-eater words no white man could ever learn to say. It was just like he expected it to mean something to Frank. Then he commences to slash away with that sword."

"Hmmm." Pike Turner consulted his thoughts in silence a moment. The name meant nothing to him. Maybe it would to Hollister, though. "And that's what you wanted to tell the colonel? All right, you'll get your chance. He'll be here in two days and you can speak to him then."

Joe Coaker beamed, relieved. "Thank you, Mr. Turner. Thank you kindly."

"It's *Captain* Turner. Don't forget that."

"Oh, no sir, no sir, Cap'in. Do . . . do you think maybe the colonel might find a place for me? Somethin' I can do? I been workin' on my draw . . . left-handed . . . and it's gettin' good. Ya wanna see?"

The man's pitiful eagerness amused Pike Turner. No doubt, once he'd delivered the message, Hollister would order Coaker disposed of. "No, too much noise at night. Save it for the colonel." To the others, he commanded, "We better turn in, boys. Tomorrow's gonna be a long day."

Tanaka Tom Fletcher rode out of Gila Bend, not eastward in the direction of Tucson, but due south toward the small village of Ajo. Odd name for a town, he reflected, recalling that it was Spanish for "garlic." Tom's familiarity with Spanish began in the Philippines and he had opportunity to improve in the language later on through conversations with priests visiting in Japan. He had journeyed to the Mogollon Rim, looking around the site of the supposed Apache raid, his clever eyes finding more than one indication that white men had been behind it. In the bathhouse-barbershop in Globe, an old copy of the Phoenix *Sun* carried an advertisement regarding sale of a valuable goldmining property belonging to one Colonel Edward Hollister.

Tom Fletcher rode as fast as possible through the dangerous canyons, ever descending until he could strike out rapidly across the flats between the Superstition Mountains and Phoenix. When he arrived, he could hardly contain his disappointment upon learning that Colonel Hollister had departed several days before, closing his office and giving up his suite at the Wheymeyer Hotel. Inquiring around the neighborhood, Tom came upon useful news.

At the livery stable, the proprietor allowed that: yes, Colonel Hollister did rent a brougham from him, with a fine pair of dapple-grays drawing it. Far as he knew, the colonel headed out toward Gila Bend. Tom wasted no time in cutting tracks in the same direction. Again, he faced disappointment. No one in Gila Bend had heard of or knew any Colonel Hollister. The name didn't appear on the register at the town's only hotel and no such striking a set of harness animals as the dapple-grays had been seen in town since the territorial governor had been there following an Apache uprising some years past. From the ferret-eyed, Mexican bartender of a small cantina, though, Tom learned of a number of hard-eyed, tough-looking men who had ridden south, toward Ajo. Their leader was a man they called Pike. Scant lead at best, but all he had to follow at the time. So, on he went.

Arising early, as was his custom, Harvey Lester laboriously dragged his wheeled cart to the deep, hand-dug community well in the center of Ajo, and filled the wooden barrel. Then he returned to his house and watered the plants in his small kitchen garden. Twice a day, at sunrise and sunset, he performed this task, taking pleasure in watching the miracle of growth as much as in the crisp, flavorful vegetables it provided for his table. This morning, however, his solitary routine was interrupted by the sudden arrival of two dozen grim-faced, hard-eyed men.

Thundering in on lathered mounts, the riders spread out through the town like a line of skirmishers. A veteran of the Army of the Potomac, Harvey noted this with the clinical detachment of an expert. He set aside his tin dipper and walked to his split-rail fence to observe their further actions.

Pike Turner and two men wheeled their horses to a halt in front of the marshal's office. The clamor of their arrival had drawn the gray-haired, pot-bellied lawman from his cot inside, yawning and stretching and slipping up a suspender strap. Rubbing at the gravel in one sleep-blurred eye, he inquired as to the strangers' business.

Turner responded with a bullet in the lawdog's chest. His draw, smooth and faultless, came so swiftly that the marshal didn't have time to remove his fist from his eyesocket before he was slammed back against the adobe wall of his office. There he hung a few moments, then slid downward to a sitting position. Dirty-gray smoke still curled from the muzzle of Pike's Remington as he waved it in the air, a circular motion that called those in sight to him.

"All right, boys. Let's get started. You three know what to do. Hit the bank, make sure to clean out everything. If it ain't open yet, open it. We'll find the banker and drag him over to lend a hand. Don't worry about anyone gettin' away, troops are covering all ways out."

After the others went about their tasks, Turner motioned to the two remaining. "Get down to the livery and check on the wagon detail. Make sure enough transport is being arranged for our needs."

"Right, Captain," came a curt reply. The men rode off.

Pike Turner pulled a fat turnip watch from his vest pocket. Popping open the cover, he consulted the time. Right on schedule, he saw with satisfaction. If everything continued as it had so far, the town would be theirs in another half hour.

Chapter Nine

Long shadows cast dark bars across the main street of Ajo by the time Tom Fletcher reached the small village. Behind him the orange-red ball of a bloated, late afternoon sun hung suspended above the craggy hills of the near horizon. The efforts of Pike Turner's troops earlier that day were not noticeable to him as his tired Morgan clopped through hock-deep dust in the main street. Harvey Lester observed his arrival and thought to himself, "Goddamn, another one of them."

Tanaka Tom reined up in front of the livery stable and dismounted. "Stable and feed for one night. Grain him."

"That'll be four bits, mister. How about the mule?"

"I'll unsaddle him and you can run him in the corral."

"That'll be two bits more."

Tom dug coins from his pocket and handed them to the stablehand. He removed the loaded packsaddle from the big, gray mule and put it on a sawhorse in a dusty corner of the building. Taking from it his *daisho* (two swords)—the *katana* and *ho-tachi*—he crossed the street to a door where a sign advertised rooms for rent. In passing, he noticed an unusual amount of bustling activity, wagons being loaded at several establishments along the main drag. At each location, one or more hard-eyed gunslingers seemed to be supervising the work. Several persons he encountered gave him strange looks, some of them hostile. Tom's curiosity rose. He arranged for a room and then headed for the barbershop for a bath and shave.

After a long soak in a hot tub, during which, for an

80

extra twenty-five cents, his clothes had been washed and quickly dried in the sere desert air, he entered the front of the shop, placing his two blades, in their case, in an umbrella stand made of a large, hollowed out, desicated saguaro cactus trunk. He seated himself in the chair and relaxed while the barber draped him in a blue, pin-striped cloth and began whipping up lather in a thick, crockery mug.

"Sure a lot goin' on here," Tom observed offhand.

One of Turner's men, placed there to watch the barber's loose tongue, eyed Tom closely. "You're new around here, ain't you?"

"Just rode in. You got a law here against askin' questions?"

"No. Only I wondered as how you hadn't heard about the, ah, gold strike."

"Gold?" Tom half rose, causing the barber's hand to slip nervously.

"Yep. Supposed to be a real *Golconda*. Ain't that right?" he directed the question to the nervous hairbutcher, as his hand moved casually toward his gun butt.

"Y-yes, sir. That's the truth. Supposed to be richer than that find in Colorado, at Cripple Creek."

"That a fact?" Tom hadn't missed the hard-eyed man's unconscious move for his six-gun. It fired his curiosity and gave him more questions to ask, at the right time.

"Oh, yes yes indeed." The barber finished stropping and with a hand that trembled slightly, applied the razor to Tom's face.

"Funny how gold touches people," the gunslinger said, his hand drawing away from his sidearm. "Folks hereabout figure on makin' their fortunes, chasin' out there and strikin' it rich."

"Good luck to 'em," Tom commented lightly. "I don't figure on joining them."

"That's a good idea, mister. A right good idea." The gunhawk's ominous tone gave Tom something more to think on.

His shave completed, Tanaka Tom discovered that

Ajo did not afford a restaurant in addition to the usual cluster of saloons. Each barroom advertised a free lunch of sorts and in one, the largest, a man could sit down to a full, hot meal. Tom seated himself at a small table, ordered a mug of beer and asked for someone from the kitchen so he could get fed.

A pop-eyed, agitated little Chinese, dressed in a black mandarin gown, slipper-shoes and small, pillbox hat shuffled with tiny steps to his table, washing his hands in the air, a servile, ingratiating look of eagerness to-please distorting his smooth, yellow-brown features even more. At least, Tom thought, he might be able to get an edible meal. In a low, commanding voice, one of samurai hauteur toward an inferior—for so the Chinese had been considered for centuries by the inhabitants of Nippon—he demanded a bowl of rice, some steamed vegetables, and slivers of fish, marinaded in sweet soya sauce.

Rather than any sign of resentment at this officious manner, the short Chinese seemed overjoyed at coming upon someone who spoke a language near enough to his own to be familiar, and with whom he could converse. Bowing profusely, his face rounded into beaming smiles, he jabbered away in a trader's lingua franca understood by both.

"It shall be as you wish, noble sir. All will be made ready. Of course, this will take some time. If the noble lord of Nippon will forebear, he shall be granted his every wish. In the meanwhile, would he desire some genuine *cha*? Savory *Keemun,* ordered expressly for the use of this unworthy one's family."

Tanaka Tom nodded his approval. Service like this made him feel almost at home. The little Chinese scurried away to place the order, leaving Tom with a satisfactory sense of expectation. At the long bar, which was filling with customers with the onset of evening, the byplay had not been missed by several dusty trail hands.

"By God, that's the first time I ever seen that flat-faced Chink treat anyone like more'n dirt. You see that, Red?"

"Sure did. Whatever that feller said to him in that

jabber talk sure scared the be-jesus outta him. Oh-oh, here comes trouble."

Several of Pike Turner's men, off duty now, swaggered through the tall batwings, making straight for the bar. Eyes downcast, customers parted to make room for them. There was no air of celebration among these hardcases. They drank with the same grim concentration they used to survey the occupants of the cantina. A short while later, Pike Turner strolled in.

He looked a cut above the others in the room, though Tanaka Tom recognized him immediately as a gunslinger. Turner's clothes denoted quality and care, and his strange, yellow-brown eyes took in everyone in the room before he took a step beyond the entrance. When he did, it was to move directly toward Tom Fletcher. He was tall, broad shouldered, and whip-cord lean so that his walk had an undulating motion about it. When he smiled his thin, bloodless lips parted to reveal white, even teeth.

"Howdy. Name's Turner, Pike Turner. Welcome to Ajo." Turner had consumed a bit more liquor than usual and, with his orders to make everything look normal he overrode his accustomed caution about giving his real name.

"Hello, Mr. Turner. And thank you. First friendly voice I've heard." Sudden intuition made Tom refrain from giving his name.

Turner laughed and pushed back the brim of his gray, flat-crowned, *sombrero de corta*. "Lot of excitement in town. You know how people are at a time like this."

"The gold rush, eh?"

"The same. Though chasin' that will-o'-the-wisp is not for me. I prefer a surer way of makin' my money."

"I'm sure you do," Tom replied dryly.

"Staying long in Ajo?"

"No. Just passing through."

Turner smiled at this. "Fine. Fine. Well, enjoy your evening, mister . . . I don't believe I got your name?"

"No, you didn't."

"Ah . . . I, ah, see. Have a good time and, ah, I'll

83

be seeing you again." Turner's oddly colored eyes glowed with sudden anger at his being crossed, but he did nothing. Hollister's orders that everything in Ajo remain, at least on the surface, as though business went as usual restrained him from using fists or six-gun as he was wont to do.

"No doubt." Tom's comment was addressed to Turner's departing back.

Chen-yi brought the tea, introducing himself as he set it down. "Only short time now. Soon bring you most enormous feast." He bent closer, speaking softly. "That man plenty-much bad. He not from Ajo. He come this morning . . . many men . . . much trouble."

"Oh? How do you mean?"

Chen-yi took a quick glance over his shoulder. Pike Turner and three of his men were closely watching what went on at Tom Fletcher's table. "Not talk now. Too much danger. Nobody can say nothing. You come kitchen, much late tonight, I tell."

Tanaka Tom sipped at his tea, wondering about this new revelation. Could it be possible he had stumbled into Hollister's latest enterprise . . . or perhaps his lair . . . after this long ride the length of Arizona? Hollister had been heading this way, though he'd not shown himself in Gila Bend. Would he now be able to end his journey of vengeance? Pike Turner's name, he reminded himself, also appeared on General Tomlinson's list. It had been this, the mention of the man's name, that had cautioned him not to give his own. It appeared that his karma had led him to this nest of vipers and delivered into his hands an opportunity to wipe out a great many of them at one time. He would think on this, make plans. To do so, though, he would need to know more about what Turner and his men were doing here, get some idea of his strength. Most important, he would have to keep out of the man's sight. He still had no answer to his questions when his food arrived.

Taking his utensil case from the right side of his *obi*, Tanaka Tom removed the ivory chopsticks and began to work on the steaming dishes placed before him with a proud flare by Chen-yi. Each item, done to perfection, delighted him. The food reminded him of his home in Japan and gave him an unaccustomed enjoyment of the meal. He gave it his full attention, failing to notice the thoughtful, suspicious look on Pike Turner's face.

"Take a look over there," Turner told the man standing next to him. "That feller eatin' like a Chinee. Sure could be the one Joe Coaker was tellin' us about. What you think?" Had he been able to see them, Tanaka Tom's swords would have given Turner all the proof he needed. Since they were uncomfortable to wear while sitting in a chair, Tom had removed them and rested the blades against the wall, out of sight. Turner quickly downed his shot of whiskey.

"I'm gonna go look up Joe. You come along. We'll bring him back here to find out for sure."

After he finished dinner, Tanaka Tom strolled over to the livery stable. He looked in on his Morgan stallion and saw that, true to his word, the stableman had provided a generous portion of oats and cracked corn. Tom killed time fiddling around with his packsaddle until the hard-eyed gunfighter type who sat at the open double doors of the barn dropped his chair back onto four legs and rose, rounding the building to relieve himself.

"I hear you have lots of trouble here in Ajo." Tom addressed his soft-voiced statement to the stable owner.

"Oh, Lord, we got more'n any man needs."

"Tell me about it."

"They rode in at first light. They just . . . took over."

"Why didn't the law do something about it?"

"Three of 'em cornered the marshal. Killed him straight off. Then they . . . well, they got control of the whole place. We can't do nothin' either. They confiscated all the guns in town right after Marshal Butler got his and left us helpless."

"How many? How big a gang is it?"

The liveryman started to answer, then turned pale as

he saw the gunman returning from his call of nature. "Aah, don't need to worry none, mister. You can see they're gettin' the best of care."

Tanaka Tom sensed the approach of the other man. "Yes. You did a good job. But you can't blame a feller for bein' concerned, right? Now, I am going to be leaving right early in the morning . . . before first light. You might have that mule loaded up by say . . . two . . . three o'clock?" Unseen by the gunslinger, Tom indicated one o'clock with a finger.

"You bet, mister. Whatever you say."

"Good." Tom Fletcher walked away before Turner's man could think of any questions to ask him.

Crossing the street again, Tom Fletcher entered a different saloon from the one where he'd dined. A careful look assured him that only one of Pike Turner's men kept watch. He stepped to the bar and leaned casually against the curved end. Setting aside the glass he had been industriously polishing, the bartender came down to where Tom waited.

"What'll you have?"

"Beer." Tom took a five-dollar gold piece from his pocket and dropped it on the polished bartop. When the apron returned with a foam-capped mug, Tom pointed to the money. "And I need a little information."

Glancing apprehensively beyond Tom's shoulder at the lone gunman, sitting at a corner table methodically drinking his way through a bottle of rotgut, the barman paled. "Are you crazy? I got nothin' to say to nobody." He sped away to make change and return it to his customer.

Undaunted, Tom sipped the brew. If not from this one, then he'd learn what he needed from another. He took a second, long pull of the beer, set the mug down. His black eyes glittered appreciatively as an overly made-up, scantily clad saloon girl made her way toward him.

"Hello, handsome. You know, you're a good lookin' hunk of man."

Tom kept his tone flat. "That's what they all say."

Rich, genuine laughter bubbled up to the girl's lips. Under the thick rouge and powder, Tom could see that she was young, much younger than he had at first believed. She flicked a provocative, pink tip of tongue across even, white teeth, and placed a slim, unwrinkled hand on his sun-browned forearm. "You're all right, mister, I'll tell you that. I like a man with a sense of humor."

"Call me Tom. Can I buy you a drink?"

"I thought you'd never ask." Again, the throaty, sincere laugh rose to her lips. "I'm Monique, Tom."

"Seems to be a lot of strangers in town."

"More than anybody wants, if you want to know the truth."

"Oh? I thought that would make good business." Tom placed money on the bar as the apron approached bearing two glasses of amber fluid.

"From this bunch?" Monique's words were cynical, resigned. She leaned closer, lips brushing Tom's ear as she spoke. "They're more interested in loot than love, if you know what I mean."

"No. Tell me more."

"Not here." Monique tossed off the liquor in her glass and glanced at the hard-drinking gunslinger. "Let's go to my room. Ain't no way they interfere with normal business like that."

"I'm your man, Monique." Tom drained his glass, linked arms with the girl and started for the stairs.

"In more ways than one, Tom. In more ways than one."

Finding Joe Coaker took considerable time. Pike Turner and his sergeant checked every saloon, the marshal's ofice, and the bathhouse behind the barbershop. At last they located one man, more sober than his companions, who remembered Coaker's departure.

"Said he was goin' to some place called, ah, Fat Hattie's."

They found Fat Hattie's, a tumble-down shack, looking more disreputable than anything else in Ajo, at the edge of town. A stench of unwashed bodies, mildewed clothes, and rotting garbage permeated the air. At a nod from Turner, the sergeant raised one big foot and kicked in the door. Joe Coaker, his naked body glistening with sweat, lay rutting atop an equally sweaty, grotesquely fat woman who whooped and hollered her enjoyment of their coupling. From a sleeping loft, built halfway up one wall, a flock of mop-headed youngsters turned from watching the spectacle to look at the sudden arrivals, their grime-encrusted faces wide-eyed with fright.

"Get your clothes, Joe. We've got a job for you."

"Aw, hell, Captain, you sure know how to spoil a feller's fun for him."

"Hop to it, this is important."

"I'm comin', Cap'in. Don't you worry, be right there."

Turner and the sergeant withdrew from the shack to avoid the acrid odor. Absently, Pike Turner wondered if Joe Coaker possessed enough subtlety or intelligence to have deliberately contrived a double entendre. No, he decided. Joe Coaker was as stupid and greed-driven as he appeared. An animal satisfying animal instincts. Two minutes later, Coaker joined them, a sheepish look on his face.

"Onliest woman in town who'd take a second look at a feller maimed like I am. Whooee! Got herself seven kids an' no two o' 'em with the same pappy. But mighty accomodatin', she is. And grateful? Lord o' Goshen, is she grateful."

Turner ignored the little outlaw's bragging. "Got someone you should take a look at. Might be you'll get your chance at revenge sooner than you thought."

Bolting the door securely behind them, Tanaka Tom turned to find Monique slipping out of her brief, saloon girl costume. "What's all this for?"

"Anyone comes up those stairs with one of the girls has to shell out hard cash. So I figured you might as well get the pleasure along with the price."

By then she had removed all her clothing and Tom saw that her flesh was warm and smooth, firm with youth. The make-up had indeed robbed her of years.

Without its garish façade, she would be a young and beautiful woman. She pirouetted on tip-toe, brazenly displaying all her charms, but with an almost coy air. Despite his interest in information rather than sex, Tanaka Tom felt himself becoming aroused.

Observing this, Monique crossed the floor and together, fumblingly, they began undressing him. Soft moans and gentle cooing sounds came from deep in the girl's throat as he revealed more and more of Tom's body. Her delight in his boldly thrusting manhood, when she exposed it, made her go weak in the knees.

Tom picked up Monique and carried her to the bed, tossing her there like a discarded bundle. Quickly he joined her, surrendering himself to a mounting passion. He entered the girl roughly, taking her almost by force the first time. In the brief, violent encounter his energy was soon spent and he lay beside Monique, relaxed and happy. A smile curled his lips a moment before he spoke.

"Tell me all you can about Pike Turner and his men."

Monique pressed fingers to his mouth. "Later, after we've both gotten what we want."

Their second mating took much longer, a languid, dream-like, co-mingling from which they emerged both victor and vanquished. Contentment settled on them and they rested.

Monique had only begun to tell Tanaka Tom all she knew about Pike Turner when someone kicked in the door.

Chapter Ten

At the same moment that Tom Fletcher and Monique started for the girl's room, Pike Turner and Joe Coaker entered the saloon. Of necessity, to climb the stairs, Tom's back was to the doorway and he failed to see the man he'd encountered before, in Washout. Coaker, however, needed only one glance.

"It's him!" he excitedly told Turner. "That sword, that . . . that sissy lookin' thing around his waist, the funny haircut . . . sure's a polecat stinks, that's the same man!"

Pike Turner placed a hand on his sergeant's shoulder. "Go round up some of the boys. Tell 'em we've got Frank Tollar's killer cornered at the Lost Dutchman saloon."

Joe Coaker fidgeted impatiently at the bar while the men came in, one or two at a time. When a half dozen had gathered, Pike Turner nodded his satisfaction. He called them together and laid out his plan.

"You two, take the back way. Marv, Hiram, you watch the stairs here. Dave, Sam, come with us." He turned to the barkeep. "What room would that pair that just went up be usin'?"

"Number nine, mister, at the far end of the hall."

"Let's move out," Turner ordered.

In the upper hall, the four men moved quietly, on tip-toe, toward the distant room. When they reached their goal, Pike Turner used hand signals to indicate that Dave was to kick open the door and the rest would follow him into the room. Beefy, barrel-shaped Dave made ready and, at a sign from Turner, slammed his size eleven boot into the door, an inch below the knob.

90

The latch gave with a pop like a shot and the panel flew inward. Off balance, Dave stumbled into the room. Sam and Joe jammed together in the doorway in their eagerness to get at the man inside.

Naked, Tom Fletcher sprang from the bed, both hands flashing toward his *obi*, which he had laid close by. His left arm snapped back, two *tonki* darts clutched in his hand, while his right shook the *katana* blade free from its scabbard. Monique screamed, struggling to cover herself with a thin, use-grayed sheet as Tanaka Tom flicked his left arm forward releasing the *tonki*.

A shot exploded in the room an instant before the thin slivers of steel entered Dave's vast belly. The burly man cried out in pain, dropped his revolver and clutched at his gut. Then the spasms began and he fell, writhing, to the floor. Joe Coaker and Sam surged into the narrow, cell-sized cubicle, crowding it even more. They stumbled over Dave's body giving Tanaka Tom time to reach the chair where he'd laid his clothes. Pike Turner added to the congestion by entering on the heels of the other two.

In such close quarters, with heaving bodies jammed against each other, Tom could not effectively use his sword. The others could hardly risk a shot. Fists began to fly. Tom took one stout punch on the point of his shoulder, rolled with it, and went in under the next one, driving a *furi-zuki* wedge-hand blow deep into the soft flesh under Joe Coaker's ribs.

Air and a spew of sour-smelling liquor gushed out of the little outlaw and he fell to the floor, out of the fight. Outnumbered by armed, determined men, fighting at such close quarters as to deny him any advantage, Tom opted for flight. He snatched up his clothes and weapons, using the chair beneath them to break out the window. Slashing left and right, he splinted the double-hung sash and sent it spinning toward the ground behind the shattered glass. Executing a short, chopping swing with the *katana*, that parted cloth on Sam's shirt front and drew blood from his chest, Tom bought time enough to leap onto the sill.

Tanaka Tom heaved his burdens over a low parapet

onto the flat roof and grasped the wooden facade tightly, preparing to vault over. Sam staggered away, a sheet of crimson running over his pale skin, giving Pike Turner a clear line of sight on the window. Pike triggered off a round as Tom Fletcher sprang out and upward.

Tom felt a searing pain along the outer side of his left thigh as he swung away from the gaping window. The bullet gouged out a strip of flesh. It bled profusely, but did little serious damage. In an instant Tanaka Tom landed on the rooftop. Pike Turner's head and shoulders thrust out through the window below and he shouted to men guarding the rear of the building.

"Look sharp, boys! He's on th . . ." Tanaka Tom's *katana* flashed downward, cutting off Turner's words as effectively as it did most of the crown of the outlaw's hat. Pike Turner jerked inward with a startled curse. Tom had bought himself a little more time.

He used it to slide into his trousers and boots, fastening his *obi* around his middle and tucking the lightweight flannel shirt into it for the time being. He adjusted the two scabbards on his left and resheathed his *katana*. He could feel blood washing down his leg, but ignored the burning pain, pushing it aside in order to make good his escape. He crossed to the opposite side of the saloon roof, and peered down at a lower building beside it. Not much of a drop, he decided, a little more than five feet. He swung his legs over the parapet, pushed off, and let go.

Tom landed safely, if a bit more noisily than he would have liked. Immediately, he headed for the far side, putting more distance between him and the Lost Dutchman saloon where Pike Turner attempted to organize his men for pursuit. Tom's luck held. No one was in sight at ground level of this building, which he now recognized as the Butterfield stage office. He swung over the edge, letting himself hang full length, then let go. He hit the ground on the balls of his feet and rolled to the right, absorbing shock and momentum harmlessly. He got up and hurried through the alleyway toward the distant livery. A slight limp hindered him, but not enough to aid those who sought him.

"You picked a funny hour to be goin' anywhere, mister," the armed guard at the stable declared as Tom entered. "You best get it cleared with Captain Turner before you leave."

The tough, young outlaw's decision became the last words he would ever speak. The sharp, slanted tip of Tanaka Tom's *katana*-shaped *tanto* fighting knife entered flesh, ripping across the gunslinger's abdomen and upward, disemboweling him, shock rendering him unconscious before he could cry out. Hot, sticky blood splashed all over Tom's arms. He let the lifeless body slip gently to the ground and washed off in a bucket beside the office door. From inside a figure moved in the dim light and Tom tensed.

"Figgered you'd be leavin' in a hurry, youngster. Yer pack mule's all saddled and ready and so's that good lookin' Morgan of yours."

"Thank you. I appreciate that."

"You . . . kill that gunhawk?" Tom nodded. "I'd be beholden if you'd drag him outside, so's the blame don't fall on me." Tanaka Tom did as the old man asked. When he returned, the stable owner had yet more to say.

"Was I you, I'd go out the back way. There's a dry wash 'bout a hundred yards from the rear of the corral. No one should see you if you take that route."

"I am, again, in your debt."

"Think nothin' of it. Best git while the gittin's good."

Tom Fletcher led his animals quietly around the edge of the corral and down into the draw. Limping, his wound more painful now, he walked a mile from town before throwing himself gratefully into the saddle. He had to come back, to even the score with Pike Turner and maybe get a chance at Colonel Hollister. To do so, he had to survive long enough to do it on his own terms. And that meant that first he had to hole up somewhere and care for his wound.

Wearily, reacting to his blood loss, Tanaka Tom started off across the desert without plan or destination.

Chapter Eleven

"All right! All right! Quiet down. Now, we can't all go ridin' out after this miserable son. We have a mission to complete here in Ajo." Pike Turner addressed his men, assembled at the main intersection of Ajo. "Joe Coaker here knows what he looks like. He'll be headin' up the bunch looking for this Fletcher."

Swelled with his sudden importance, Joe swaggered a little as he stepped forward. "The cap'n here says I can take five men. He's chosen two of them; Nimrod Jackson an' Ace Weller. I'll take Ted Harmes, you Keller, and Laird. No use tryin' to track him in the dark. We'll meet at the livery stable and start off from there at dawn."

"Remember," Pike Turner added as a final instruction. "Nobody's going to complain if you bring back a carcass instead of a breathin' man."

Reeling in the saddle, Tom Fletcher tried to focus uncooperative eyes on a small, yellow square of light in the distance . . . a house, no doubt someone's small ranch. It meant people and a chance to rest up. Although once clear of town, Tanaka Tom had taken time to bandage his wound, it continued to seep blood. Added to that which he lost through his exertions to escape, he was weakened considerably. As the Morgan plodded onward, the dark shapes of several buildings began to loom out of the night. Tom spotted a low, white, picket fence in time to prevent his horse from stumbling into it. Dismounting proved an ordeal in itself.

Clammy sweat broke out on Tom's skin as he swung

a leg over, biting back an involuntary gasp of pain as full weight came on his wounded thigh. He lowered himself to the ground and negotiated the gate. He stumbled onto the porch and rapped at the door. A curtain brushed aside and Tom caught a momentary glimpse of a fair-skinned, young face. Somewhat muffled, he heard a feminine voice, calling.

"Paw . . . there's someone here! He's been hurt."

A few moments passed, which seemed an eternity to Tom, then the door opened amid the grumbling complaint of a male voice. "Dadgumit, Emmy. How many times have I told you to be careful?"

"I got the Spencer down, Paw."

"But you didn't have it cocked. Give it here." A big framed man filled the open doorway and Tom looked down the huge .54 caliber muzzle of a Spencer rifle. The grizzled rancher studied the weaving man on his doorstep. "State yer business, stranger."

"I've been shot. At Ajo. I need a place to rest . . . take care of my wound."

Eyes narrowing suspiciously, the old man studied Tom. "You one of the gunslicks we heard rumor had ridden into Ajo?"

"No. They're the ones who shot me." Tom could almost feel the tension relax. The old man grunted and stepped aside.

"Here, take the rifle, Emmy." Tom stumbled over the threshold, which seemed a mile high. The rancher surged forward. "Let me help you, mister."

Tom found himself supported across the floor to a large couch, where the rancher lowered him gently onto his uninjured side. Tom gazed upward into bright, blue eyes above rosy, youthful cheeks. A girl of about sixteen stood near the divan, arms and legs akimbo, a heavy Spencer rifle cradled in the crook of one elbow. Her look of curious concern bloomed into a blush and she smiled shyly when she realized his eyes were open again and turned on her.

"Get them trousers off him, Emmy, while I go fetch the medicine chest."

"Paw!" the girl cried, scandalized. "I'm . . . I'm

95

. . . I mean he's a man . . . an' a stranger and I'm
. . . a woman."

"An' this is an emergency, girl. Do as I say."

"Yes, sir." Hanging the Spencer on pegs over the
fireplace, Emmy knelt beside Tom Fletcher. After a
couple of unsuccessful tries, she mastered the intricacies
of his *obi* and removed it. She undid his belt buckle and
the buttons of his Levis.

"Oh! Ooooh, Paw!" she cried out, flushing a furious
red at the discovery that in his haste to escape Pike
Turner's killers, Tom had neglected to put on underclothes.

"What you actin' so all fired squeamish-innocent
about? 'Tain't nothin' you ain't seen before. You gave
your little brother a bath from the day he was borned
'til this year, didn't you?"

Emmy tried to protest her father's no-nonsense point
of view. "But . . . but this is different. He's a stranger
and a growed man."

"He's a growed, wounded man, I might point out,
missy. Now you go stir this smooth while I cut away the
old bandage." Clucking to himself, half amused at his
daughter's embarrassment, he squatted beside Tom. Using a heavy pair of old, well-worn scissors, he cut away
the blood-sopped rags with which Fletcher had bandaged himself.

"Mean lookin' son of a gun. Messy, though not too
deep. We'll have you mended up in no time." With a
piece of cotton waste he dabbed at the slow seep of
blood welling up in the bullet groove while he continued to talk. "Tell me, is it true what we heard from a
Mezkin kid who rode through here early this mornin'?
Did an outlaw gang take over Ajo?"

"Only too true, Mr. . . ah?"

"Hayes. George Benjamin Hayes. Friends call me
Ben."

"Ben it is. There are two dozen gunmen, organized
into some sort of military-like unit, in Ajo. They are
under the command of a man named Pike Turner.
Turner is a former infantry officer in the Union Army.

96

They are looting the town of everything valuable, but no one seems to know why or where they are planning to take their plunder."

"Well, my guess wouldn't be any better than anyone else's. From what you say, you're lucky to get out with only a nick in your hide. Ah, here comes Emmy now."

The girl handed her father the small crockery jar he had given her, eyes averted from Tom's nakedness. The contents had an evil smell and, as Ben Hayes scooped up a large glob on two fingers, he continued to talk in an encouraging tone.

"This will stop the bleedin' for sure. Should heal you up with hardly a scar. Hold on to your hair, though. It stings like a hat full of hornets."

True to the rancher's words, a burning, tingling sensation radiated through Tom's body from his wound as Ben applied a liberal coating of the brown-amber, foul smelling salve. Ben wiped his hands and applied a folded strip of gauze, then wrapped a bandage around Tom's thigh.

"Stay off of that for as long as you can. Change the dressin' twice a day and don't get any water on it until that salve has soaked into your skin."

"Are you a doctor?"

Ben snorted. "Me? Heck no. Everybody who's lived in these parts for more'n ten years knows a little medicine, or they don't survive. You could use somethin' to build up your blood. Emmy, bring us a pitcher of water and that bottle of whiskey in the cupboard. And fry up some of that liver we had left from supper. Just braise it and get it hot on the inside." He turned back to Tom. "Best thing for a feller low on blood. Now. There's somethin' that's got me powerful curious. Them swords of yours?"

"They are the symbols of authority and the main weapons of the samurai warrior class, the knights of Japan. I have lived most of my life in that country and there I am a member of a ranking samurai clan." While Emmy continued the task of preparing a meal and her father listened in fascination, Tom Fletcher talked of his past and explained his mission of vengeance against Edward Hollister and his men. When he finished, Ben Hayes had several shrewd questions.

"You figure to get revenge on all those who were at your family's plantation? Be kind of hard, goin' up against trained soldiers without a gun, won't it?"

"We samurai are familiar with firearms, Ben. But they are looked down on as the tools of . . . ah, Western barbarians." Tom smiled ruefully. "Though I have recently come to appreciate their effectiveness."

"How's that? Your wound?"

"No." Tom went on to tell him about the stage holdup he surprised in progress. Ben only shook his head.

"I'll swear. You can find more damned trouble than any five men I know. Well, looks like your eats are ready. Can you make it into the kitchen?"

Tom started to rise when a voice from the inner doorway interrupted them. "What's happened, Paw? Who's this?" A tousle-headed boy of seven or eight stood just inside the room, his face slack from sleep, knuckling one eye.

"This is Mr. Fletcher, son. He's been hurt. We're puttin' him up for the night. You run up to your room and bring down a pillow and blanket. You can sleep on the couch."

"Yes, sir." The boy padded away on bare feet, still not fully cognizant of his surroundings.

Tom ate—discovering to his surprise that for some reason, perhaps his blood loss, he relished the nearly raw liver despite his years of eating little meat—then slept until mid-morning. A low rumble of voices wakened him. He dressed and went downstairs. Stiffness had settled into his left leg, but the pain had diminished considerably. He found his host seated alone at the kitchen table, a heavy crockery mug of coffee neglected in one hand, with a dark, worried expression clouding his face.

"Something wrong, Ben?"

"One of my neighbor's hands came over. Said there's some tough-looking customers on their range, quartering back and forth like they were tryin' to cut a trail. Could be this Pike Turner isn't satisfied with you up and ridin' away."

A momentary pique flared. "Does everyone in the valley know I'm here?"

"Oh, it's not that. A long time ago, as a matter of mutual protection, we got in the habit of passin' the word any time we come across something out of the ordinary happening."

"I see. All the same, it sounds like you're right. They are searching for me. I'll be leavin' now."

"You won't make it far with that wound. Best that you stay."

"I don't wish to bring any trouble your way."

"We've dealt with a lot worse than a handful of gunfighters."

"This isn't your fight. As soon as I can saddle up, I'm leaving."

Ben rose from the table. "If you won't listen to reason, Mr. Fletcher, at least let me give you some advice." At Tom's nod, he went on. "There's a spring about seven miles west of here. It's up in the rocks, well off the trail. You can cover all approaches from there. If these gunslicks don't know the country, they'll never know it's there. In daylight you can cover your tracks well enough they can't trail you there either. Best take along the rest of this salve, too. My only worry is that you can make it that far without startin' your wound to bleedin' again."

"That's *my* worry, Ben . . . and thanks."

Joe Coaker sat his mount, frowning in concentration. Tracking Fletcher proved harder than he'd expected. They'd come upon a shallow stream and there lost the Morgan's hoofprints entirely. After scouring the bank in both directions, Nimrod Jackson returned at last to say that he'd found occasional signs of the pack mule but nothing of the Morgan, which left him puzzled. Had Fletcher turned the animal loose as a decoy? Or was he staying close to the water, leading the critter? Which way to go? If the mule had been on its own, by now it would have stopped to graze and Jackson would have found it. Coaker smiled. Fletcher had to have been leading his pack animal. The only answer that made sense.

He called in the others and they headed along the stream. Half an hour later, they came up over a low rise and spotted a neatly laid out ranch headquarters, the outbuildings painted and carefully tended. Flogging his horse's rump with his big, floppy hat, Nimrod Jackson galloped up to Joe Coaker.

"Mis'er Coaker, Mis'er Coaker, I done got the trail clear as all git out now. He done rode down to that there ranch."

"Good going, Nimrod. What say we pay those folks a little visit?"

By the time Tom Fletcher began to set up camp beside the small spring, the effects of his wound and the exertion of his travels began to tell heavily on him. He had ridden well past the landmarks described by Ben Hayes as locating the turnoff point for the spring. Carefully selecting a hard, stony stretch of trail, where the ground would not take hoofprints, he had left the road on a large slab of rock. Tom rode to the far uphill end of the sheet and dismounted. Using a file he altered distinctive marks on two of the Morgan's shoes and one on the pack mule. Then he mounted and rode off toward the top of the ridge.

On the other side, out of sight of the trail, Tanaka Tom took a circuitous route back to the spring. He unsaddled his animals and hobbled them so they could graze on the sparse grass around the spring. Each task required even greater effort on his part and he began to appreciate Ben Hayes's observation on his physical condition. An oily, chill dampness covered his body, yet he felt feverish. After rigging his oilskin coat as a sunshade, he spread his saddle blanket and dropped wearily onto it. At last he could relax his conscious effort to hold back the growing weakness that threatened to overwhelm him. He took a deep, refreshing drink from

100

his canteen and, sighing wearily, fell back on his impro-
vised pallet, arms flopping widely.

A huge, red-brown scorpion, intent upon stinging to
death his latest victim, a small lizard, took immediate
and violent exception to the sudden, unexpected arrival
of the large, fleshy appendage that knocked the still
conscious prey away from it, allowing the lizard to
scurry to freedom. The deadly arachnid bristled and
went into its battle dance. Body quivering in a frenzy, it
elevated its sinuous tail and lashed out with the poi-
soned tip, sinking it deeply into Tom Fletcher's flesh.

Tom's reaction, swift and deadly, cost the scorpion
its life but left him with a large, painful, angry red
swelling on the inside of his left forearm. Even as he sat
looking at the sting, reaching for his *tano* knife to open
the flesh in order to suck out the poison, the potent
fluid began spreading through his system.

Cut . . . and suck . . . and spit . . . suck . . .
and spit . . . Tom's hurrying efforts seemed futile to
him as he felt a burning, itching sensation spreading up
his arm. Suck again and spit, he commanded himself.
Again! Nausea overcame him and he bent to one side,
retching weakly. His vision blurred and objects began
to swim about, seemingly detached from the ground.
His heart began to beat ever faster in his chest and his
breath came in short, arrested gasps. With a groan, he
fell on his back, unconscious.

Chapter Twelve

"Howdy. You seen a stranger around these parts? He would be ridin' a big Morgan bay, leadin' a gray pack mule." Joe Coaker sat atop his sweating horse outside the picket fence at the Hayes ranch.

Ben Hayes stood on the opposite side of the gate, at the end of his short walk, looking up at the six hard-faced, cold-eyed men. He squinted in the bright midday sun and wiped sweat from his brow with the back of one hand.

"Nope. Don't recall any such."

"Oh, come on, mister. We tracked him right here to your ranchyard. It'll go hard for you if you don't tell us what we want to know."

"You lawmen?"

Coaker laughed, a short, ugly snort, and his Colt "open top" .44 appeared in his left hand. "This here is all the authority I need. Now start talkin'."

"You can't get away with this. I've got hands here . . ."

"They're down on your south pasture chasin' cows. There's no way they could make it back here before dark even if they did hear a shot. I don't have to kill you, you know? I can gibble you up so's you spend every minute of the rest of your life in pain. Is that saddle bum you're protectin' worth that?"

"Get the hell off my land!"

"Ted. You an' Keller round up anyone else on the place. Bring 'em out front here."

Grinning, Ted Harmes came back a few minutes later, carrying a wriggling, screaming boy. Held face down by the back of his belt, Ben's son made helpless swimming motions in the air. Harmes set him on his feet beside his father. From inside the house they heard a startled yelp and a single, heavy blast.

A couple of seconds later, Jack Keller came out onto the porch, grinning. He carried Emmy Hayes from behind, arms around her waist, holding her off the ground so that she kicked and flailed uselessly at him. He deposited her next to her father and glanced at Coaker for approval. Still astride his mount, to Joe Coaker's left, Nimrod Jackson's eyes glowed with sudden interest.

"Where's your wife?"

"She . . . she's in that little cemetery yonder. She died when Tory there was born. There's just the three of us." Ben Hayes, subdued now by the roundup of his children, seemed more cooperative.

"Them things happen," Coaker acknowledged indifferently. "Now, tell us all about the man on the Morgan."

"I've got nothin' to say."

"You crazy or somethin', mister? How'd you like that boy o' yourn gut-shot? He'd take a long time dyin'."

Had it not been for the gun in Coaker's hand, Ben Hayes might have attacked the outlaw, seeking to smash and batter his face to a pulp. As it was, he nearly did so anyway, stopped only when the maimed little gunman went on in a laconic voice.

"No. I know a better way to get at your kind, mister. Take good care of this place, don't you?" Coaker's resentment of men with permanence and property sounded heavily in his voice. "Got a lot of pride in it. Shows what your real love is . . . money and possessions. Nimrod, you an' Ace go set light to that chicken house. And the hay barn, too. Hell, fire the whole damned place. Ol' stubborn here ain't gonna need it anymore."

In a few minutes the chicken house burned lustily. The almost human yelps of the dying birds were pitiful to hear and the odor of their burning feathers made a heavy, sickening stench in the air. Laughing and joking with each other, Nimrod and Ace started for the hay barn.

"You win!" Ben Hayes cried in an agonized voice. "Stop them from firing my barn and I'll tell you what I know."

"Talk fast or it goes up anyway."

"He . . . he came here. Early this morning. Watered his horse and mule and rode on out."

"Which way did he go?"

"I didn't see. Maybe he went along with the hands. Might be in Mexico by now."

Coaker made no sign to stop the burning, so Nimrod and Ace fired the barn. Flames leaped high along the walls, licking hungrily through the dry, gathered grasses inside. "My way of insurin' you're tellin' the truth, feller." Rising in his stirrups, Joe called to the arsonists. "Turn that stock out and fire them stables, too."

"Damn you, I've told you all I know!" Tears welled in Ben Hayes's eyes as he watched the destruction of all he'd slaved and struggled to build over the years.

"I'm not all too sure about that. When the boys get done there, think I'll turn that pretty daughter of yourn over to Nimrod. He's got a thing about blonde girls, the younger the better."

Ben Hayes's control snapped. With a snarl, he leaped at Joe Coaker, arms extended, fingers yearning to grasp the outlaw by the throat. "You bastard!"

Coaker smashed the butt of his revolver down on the top of Ben's head. The rancher fell, cut, bleeding and unconscious in the dirt. Eyes on the sobbing, frightened girl, Joe dismounted, leering as he walked to where Emmy stood, holding her little brother. Licking his lips, spread in a lustful grin, he reached out to take Emmy by the arm.

"Think I'll take first turn on this one myself."

"Kombahn-wa, sensi-san." The small boy, barefoot, wearing only a tightly belted *gi*, bowed low before his black-robed instructor, greeting him solemnly. His heart fluttered with momentary insecurity, as he made

104

ready to face his first opponent, Hieraga Togo, a smug, sneering bully, grossly fat for a thirteen-year-old—built like a *sūmo* wrestler—the entire class knew he hated Tanaka Tomi because of his white skin. The boy knew Hieraga would do something to hurt him, perhaps break a bone or two.

"You are to execute a *kata* using *shuto, teisho, ura ken, yoko hiji ate* and *fumikomi* techniques. *Wakarimasu ka*?" their teacher demanded before giving the signal to begin.

Oh, he understood all right. He also understood far sooner than the others how not to show pain. This would, for sure, be another of those times when this ability was tested to the fullest. He set himself, started forward . . .

. . . No! That wasn't right. His enemy was the wind, whipping up now while lightning blazed and thunder rolled in the sky. The wind and the poison that burned through his body. Water. He needed a drink. Weakened as well by hunger and blood loss, Tom Fletcher's body fought desperately to throw off the effects of the scorpion's venom. Not ordinarily fatal to a grown person, in Tom's present condition, the arachnid's sting brought death close at hand. He reached a trembling hand toward his canteen, touched it so that it wobbled and fell, spilling its precious contents onto the sand. Hours passed.

Tom burned with fever, then shook with chills as the mounting gale buffeted him over and over. He had to get help, get to a doctor. He had to reach his horse . . . his horse . . . a samurai . . .

". . . a samurai and his horse must become one and inseparable. This is the essence of *bajutsu*. Each must come to learn the wants and needs of the other. A samurai must be able to mount and dismount standing, at a walk, and at a gallop. Let us demonstrate this maxim. Tanaka Ichimara Tomi!"

The slender, dark-haired boy stood from the squatting cluster of his contemporaries, bowed low to their instructor, and walked out to the center of the exercise yard. There stood a sturdy Mongol pony, attached to a harness at the end of a long arm which permitted it to travel only in a circle. He walked alongside the nag and, flexing his knees, sprang onto the saddle pad without using his hands. Throwing his leg over, he slid off the opposite side of the animal and gave it a slap on the rump.

When the horse began to trot, he gauged its speed and ran in toward it from the right side, vaulting, one-handed, over its rump. He settled, spraddle-legged, on the pad. Clinging with only his knees, he made a full circuit of the yard. Then he swung his right leg over and dropped lightly to the ground. He scooped up a pebble and shied it off the horse's silky flank. It immediately broke into a gallop. This time he took even greater care.

Running through the dust until he matched the nag's speed and closed on it, he used both hands to vault fully onto the galloping platform. With hardly a pause, he pushed up on his splayed fingers to full arm extension and swung his body and legs around, reversing his position, and dismounting backward, dangerously close to the flying rear hoofs.

"*Banzai*! *Banzai*!" cried a number of the class. A broad grin of pride and happiness spread over Tanaka Tomi's face. Horses, he thought with smug satisfaction, were something Tommy Fletcher knew more about than the others . . .

. . . the others, the men hunting him! They would be coming. He had to get away. He could see them closing in on him. Yes! There they were, huge and black, filling the whole sky. A glaring flash of lightning blinded his pain-filled eyes as right upon it the shattering crash of thunder deafened him. The wind howled vengefully as darkness closed in.

"Storm comin'," Ace Weller pointed to the roiling, black masses towering over the desert floor.

"Looks dangerous. We don't want to get caught out in that." Joe Coaker shivered as a gust of chill wind caught at his coat.

106

"We'd better make camp. I'll look for a place while Nimrod keeps on cuttin' sign."

"You do that, Ace. You sure that fool rancher told us the truth?"

"We been readin' his tracks right along, Coaker. Don't you worry none, if he turns off, we'll know about it."

"If that storm hits between us an' him, that might not be so easy."

"Even if it's a cloudburst, we can sniff him out after. I swear that nigger's part bloodhound."

"Colored folk don't take kindly to that word, Ace."

"What's wrong with callin' one a bloodhound?" Ace asked with a perfect deadpan.

Joe Coaker laughed heartily. "You take the cake, Ace. If you don't even know what it is you said wrong, what's the use of tryin' to teach you? Get on with you, now. Let's get buttoned down in camp before we get soaked."

Chapter Thirteen

Rain. It fell in buckets and barrelfuls, soaking at first into the parched sands of the desert, splashing off the rocky hills into slender streams that gained in strength as they fell into dry creekbeds, nourished by runoff from the quickly surfeited land. The clouds seemed to hover motionless over the ground and pour out a silver-streaked deluge. And still it came, more and more rain . . .

. . . Rain fell heavily on the Shimizu Plain, wetting horses, men and all their equipment. Fourteen-year-old Tanaka Ichiwara Tomi had been allowed by his father to come along with the *Fujika rentai* for the first time. He would serve as a message runner. There had been a small uprising, a defiance of authority. Some fishing villages had turned from their traditional occupation to piracy and the shogun ordered his own regiment, the *Fujika*, to the area to visit his displeasure on the offenders. So far it had been an unimportant, routine little campaign.

The first village had been fallen upon with complete surprise. A shower of arrows had dispatched the look-outs and the samurai swarmed into the streets on their horses, exacting a bloody toll. Some of the pirates holed up in a large godown, the stone walls of the warehouse providing them momentary protection. Then Tanaka Nobunara, serving temporarily as *butaicho* of the artillery, had brought up his guns. He sent his son, Tanaka Tomi, galloping off to the squadron commander's pavillion, erected outside town, to inform him that all was in readiness.

Racing over the cobbles, made slick with the blood

of many pirates and residents, the boy rounded a corner to be suddenly confronted by three armed men. He struggled furiously to control his shying horse as he studied those threating him.

Two of them were bandy-legged fishermen, unskilled in the use of arms. Their leader, he saw, was a *ronin*, a rogue samurai, masterless and unwilling to do the honorable thing by committing *seppuku*. He had thrown in his lot with the villagers' piratical enterprise. Here, then, the boy realized, lay his greatest danger.

"Ho! Friends, now you shall hear my *katana* sing. Here is an opponent worthy of a samurai." Following his boasting, the *ronin* called out to Tanaka Tomi, as tradition decreed, his name and history. "I am Noriega Heideki, *ronin,* formerly of the Shikoku *rentai,* in service to the daimyo of Osaka. Prepare to defend your life!"

Mention of this hereditary enemy fired anger in the boy's heart. He remembered only too well his days as Tommy Fletcher, street urchin, roaming the alleyways of Edo half starved as result of the enmity of the daimyo of Osaka. He drew his *katana*, a full-sized one due to his large stature, and shouted his own defiant challenge.

"I am Tanaka Ichimara Tomi of the *Fujika rentai,* in service to the shogun. Give way or die!" Although his body had reached and surpassed the size of the average adult Japanese, his voice was still that of a small boy. The *ronin*, grinning, noticed it.

"What is this? A mere boy! Yet you draw a *katana* like a man so you shall die like one!" The *ronin* and his followers charged.

Instead of waiting to receive their charge, Tanaka Tomi drubbed his heels into his horse's ribs and lunged forward. Steel rang on steel with such force the boy thought he might lose his grip, then his war-trained steed sidestepped and once more blades met. Kneeing his mount, causing it to back obediently, he suddenly found himself with the space he needed. The *katana* whistled through the air as he brought it down into position to make a horizontal blow. Swinging the blade forward, all the weight of his arm and shoulder behind it, he swiftly and neatly struck off the *ronin's* head.

As his horse bolted through the space so quickly opened before it, Tanaka Tomi rolled his arm and delivered a backward, vertical slash that opened one pirate's back from buttocks to shoulder blades. Sudden exhilaration coursed through his young body.

"*Banzai! Banzai! Banzai!*" he shouted as he sped off down the road.

Tommy Fletcher had killed his first man—men. Considering the savage slash he gave the pirate, he had been blooded in battle. Once the skirmish was over, he was to be feasted by his adopted father and the artillery *butai*. But first, after delivering his message, the realization of his act came upon him, and he stumbled off among the slender trees and got violently sick. An affable old samurai came to him and gave him water to rinse his mouth. He also brought advice.

"It is always thus with the first one," he told the boy. "It would be inhuman not to feel something. Remember, though, a samurai's life is to fight, and in the future your stomach will glory in it as much as your heart."

Tommy wasn't all that sure, though he agreed weakly. As he hurried back to his father's artillery detachment with orders to open fire on the godown, he puzzled over the contrasting emotions warring within him. How could it be, he asked himself, that killing a man could weaken him to the point of nausea and at the same time fire him with an aching, demanding, sexual hunger?

Now, less than a week later, the campaign had ground to a soggy, muddy halt. Stalled on the Shimizu Plain by incessant rain. And more rain . . .

. . . Rain! Yes, that's what it is. Cold rain pouring down out of a black sky. Tom Fletcher opened his eyes to find the world around him swimming in a downpour. One of the infrequent flash floods that inundated sections of the Arizona desert, while leaving land on all sides of the storm bone dry. And his shivering, he discovered, came from his cold drenching in raindrops,

110

not the poison fever that had consumed him for several hours before the storm began. Glad to be alive, feeling rested and restored, Tanaka Tom threw back his head and laughed aloud, letting the huge drops fall into his open mouth. Then, as quickly as it had started, the overwhelming precipitation ended.

Silence filled the desert, broken only by the distant roar of water cascading through once-dry stream beds. Thin trickles ran here and there, to be quickly whisked out of sight under the ever thirsting sands. The sun reappeared. A few hours remained before nightfall so Tom stripped out of his sodden clothes, opened his packs, and spread out everything to dry. The sun quickly warmed his naked body as he searched through his belongings for a rolled string that, as he had hoped, had managed to stay dry. Stringing his bow, he set out to find something to eat. While he hunted, he mused over how great a meat eater he was becoming. Though necessity, as his aged instructor in martial arts had often told him, always gave birth to invention.

Tom Fletcher's pursuers hadn't fared as well in the storm as he. They had camped in the shelter of a side valley of the range of hills some three miles short of the turnoff to the spring. It hadn't looked like a creek bed—they were desert-wise enough to avoid such places—and in fact it wasn't. Yet, when the sky blackened overhead and unleashed its torrential downpour, the quickly surfeited sands rejected the massive volume of liquid and, as it gathered far above them, sent a wall of water rampaging down between the confining ledges.

In a matter of seconds they lost two pack animals and nearly all of their supplies. Rod Laird was swept away, screaming, in the flood. By the time the fury abated, there remained the prospect of a cold, hungry night on the desert and no chance to locate their quarry.

"Any tracks he may have left are wiped out now," Ace Weller complained. "That flash flood did him more good than a bag full of double eagles. I say we turn back, make our report to Cap'n Turner."

111

"No!" Joe Coaker's anxiety showed clearly on his tormented face. "That'd mean leavin' him to get away scot free. This is still our best chance of runnin' him down. And I've got a lot of getting even to do."

"Use your head, Coaker. There's no tellin' how long it would take to cut his trail again. We've got no supplies, short on livestock, and one man dead already. We don't have a choice but to go back."

Coaker turned scornful, seeking to inflame the men to his way of doing things. "All this time I thought Colonel Hollister had *men* following him. Go back if you want, you yellow bellies, but I'm stayin'."

Ace Weller's eyes grew hard, bleak, his lips twisted into a sneer. "They buried the last feller called me yellow. I was only twelve at the time."

Ted Harmes stepped between them. "There's no call to fight among ourselves. I agree with Ace, we should go back. One man's not as important as the job the colonel sent us here to do. That comes first."

Weller, his hand still stroking the butt of his six-gun, stood in frigid silence a moment longer, then turned and walked to his horse. Slowly and deliberately he began to saddle the animal, his back turned to Joe Coaker. A moment later, Ted Harmes and Jack Keller joined him. Joe stood alone, fuming in helpless fury. Only he and Nimrod Jackson remained. As the men threw a leg over their mounts, Joe gave them a parting shout.

"Tell Turner we camped here overnight. We'll move out first thing in the morning. An' we'll run that damn Fletcher to the ground before nightfall."

Tom Fletcher's hunting proved bountiful. He downed a large armadillo. He gutted the animal and roasted it whole, in its shell, over a low bed of coals. The meat tasted sweet and succulent, only the legs being stringy. He consumed all of it, along with half a dozen rice balls, washing down his meal with fresh-brewed tea. He licked clean his greasy fingers, patted his bulging stomach and belched thunderously. What, for Tom, could be considered an act of gluttony had come in answer to a consuming craving for meat.

112

His body required a great deal of protein to produce healing flesh to mend his wound. Equally drained by the scorpion's sting, debility left him nearly helpless. Like a siren call, the mysterious power of his *ki* force had made stridently clear his bodily needs to his conscious mind. Already he could feel the rich nourishment spreading through his lean frame. Sated for the time being, Tom now turned his attention to his belongings.

His clothing, blankets, and other supplies had dried sufficiently to allow him to repack the large hide folders that fitted his pack saddle, and to dress. Those tasks accomplished, he slept soundly until dawn.

A breakfast of cold rice balls and tea began Tom's day. Already he felt the strength returning to his body. He would hunt for meat again that afternoon to speed his recovery. The flesh wound in his thigh still pained slightly and he carefully redressed it with the salve and bandages given him by Ben Hayes. The scorpion sting had reduced in proportion to a walnut-sized, purple-black knot. He still felt a little light-headed, he admitted to himself, so Tom decided to spend most of the day in further rest and recovery before starting out again after Pike Turner and, hopefully through him, Edward Hollister.

In the drowsy heat of mid-afternoon, Tom discovered that fish inhabited the small pond formed by the spring. Crouching at its side, he set about catching his evening meal. To do so he used a method known to small boys in Japan for centuries.

First he smeared his hand and forearm with raw ginger root to take away the man-smell. Then he immersed it in water up to the wrist. Keeping absolutely motionless, he waited until a curious catfish undulated out of the mud and coasted silently up to the pallid, white object dangling limply in his domain. As the inquiring creature sidled up to nuzzle one finger, Tom snatched him with a blurred, lightning move.

Wriggling in furious reaction to capture, the spike-armed fish tried to impale Tom as he slipped a leather thong through mouth and gill, before returning the one pounder to its own habitat. Patiently he repeated the

113

process until he added two more finny delights to the string. Leaving them there, Tom went to his pack. He pulled out two long, narrow strips of jerked beef, provided by Emmy Hayes, and munched on them. He spent the remainder of the afternoon napping lightly. By evening he awoke with great hunger.

Fletcher cooked and ate his fill of fish, rested, then consumed the remainder. With each passing moment it seemed he could feel his renewing vitality. Exercise, he knew, would loosen his stiffened joints and the muscles of his injured leg. He thought about it as he prepared his evening ritual pot of *cha*. Dressed in his *kimono* and *gehtas*, head bare, he sat and sipped the fragrant green tea while looking far out to the west and enjoying the sunset. After finishing the *cha*, he decided, he would run through a couple of katas, using the stylized, disciplined karate drills to return suppleness to his limbs and body. He breathed in the lush, clean smell of the desert and appreciated its peaceful quiet.

Nimrod Jackson felt defeat and disappointment for the first time since Colonel Hollister and his men freed him from his slave's existence on the plantation. A natural tracker, he had to admit the scouring effect of wind and rain had totally destroyed any sign of this Fletcher's passage. As the day wore on, Joe Coaker fidgeted impatiently, growing cross and abusive. His sour comments added to Nimrod's discomfort.

"We ain't gonna find him this way, Joe," Nimrod protested. "I say we oughta ride hell for leather until we get to the other side of where the storm hit. That's where we'll find his tracks."

They had ridden slowly through the long afternoon, frequently ranging far to each side of the trail, seeking what they could not find. An hour before sunset found them only three miles beyond the turnoff for the spring neither man knew of. Still burning with eagerness to close with his enemy, Joe realized the necessity of rest for both their mounts and themselves. Reluctantly he decided on a stop for the night. While Jackson scoured up enough sparse wood for a fire, he stood, hands on

114

hips, turning slowly, his eyes scanning the far horizon. There! Back the way they had come. In those rocks . . . could that be a column of smoke?

"Hey, Nim. Look over there. See it?" Joe pointed the direction with the stubs of his severed fingers.

"Hmmm. That looks like smoke."

"You know of anyone else would be out here but us . . . and him?"

A wide, toothy white grin split the black man's face. "No, sir. Couldn't be nobody else a-tall."

"Let's ride," Joe threw over his shoulder, rushing for his horse.

Darkness had settled over the desert by the time Joe and Nimrod left their horses and began making their way quietly through the rocks to a place that overlooked Tom Fletcher's campsite. Crouched among the boulders, their eyes widened in wonder as they watched Tom go about cleaning up his tea service.

"Pssst! Joe, take a look at that dress. Is this feller one of them fancy boys like C. C. Steel?"

"I don't know him well enough to tell that, but you never know. What's he doin' now?"

"Looks like he's strippin' down."

Below them, Tom Fletcher finished packing his cooking utensils and tea set, then stepped out of his *gehtas*. He removed his *tabi* slippers and *obi* and slipped out of his kimono. Dressed only in his Japanese-style loincloth, he assumed the "horse" position to begin the first of three planned *katas* of twenty-five moves each. Three quick, deep breaths put him in tune with his *ki* and, gusting forth a high-pitched yell, he began the patterned movements.

Stepping forward on the left foot and pivoting, he delivered a *yoko geri keage* side-kick with the right to the kneecap of an unseen enemy. He continued his movement, slashing backward with a right-hand elbow blow—an *ushiro hiji ate*—followed by a side-hammer, *kea tsui*, smash that would have connected with an unprotected skull had anyone been there. At the same time, his left hand didn't remain idle.

115

Leaving the "horse" defense in an *age uke* rising forearm block, he stiffened his fingers, locking them into position. Then continuing the momentum, he slashed downward with the toughened edge in a knife-blade *shuto* chop. Whirling around he dropped into a crouch, arms crossed at the wrists in a *juji uke* "A" block. His fingers writhed as they grasped the front of an imaginary attacker's garment. Jerking downward, he thrust upward with one leg, planting his heel in the invisible stomach and flipping the opponent over his head, simulating a *tomoe-nage*. In a swirl of sand, giving another sharp *ki-ayi* yell, Tom came up and stamped furiously with one *soku-to* foot to crush a throat.

Eyes wide with confusion and superstitious fear, Nimrod Jackson hissed his words at his partner. "Lawdy! De Debbil hisself done got hold o' dat man's soul."

"For sure I've never seen any shadow boxin' like that. Maybe the sun got him? Whatever the case, it makes our job easier. C'mon. Let's take that loco hombre."

Feeling his body smoothing out into its accustomed perfect rhythm, his heart beat light and steady, Tom Fletcher swelled inside with satisfaction. The blood coursed through his veins, bringing tingling life to every part. He completed his first *kata* with perfect execution and, without a pause, moved gracefully into the second.

Strike right . . . left . . . block . . . back kick . . . block . . . pivot . . . and block . . . and . . . He froze in place as a voice came from the outer darkness.

"Hold it right there, mister. Your sissy dancin' around won't do you any good against a six-gun."

Joe Coaker and Nimrod walked into the firelight, destroying the advantage of their night sight, handguns at the ready. Both men blinked in the sudden brightness, missing the small, anticipatory smile that flickered on Tanaka Tom's lips.

"Joe Coaker, I believe." Tom let the words out in a soft purr. "I see your earlier instruction didn't take. Now I'll have to give you both a lesson in karate."

"The onlyist thing you'll show us is how to die. This is for Frank Tollar!" Joe should have known better than to telegraph his shot like that, but perhaps he had a learning difficulty as a child. The hammer of his Colt fell, the cartridge detonated and the bullet sped through empty space where a moment before Tanaka Tom Fletcher had stood. Surprise at missing at such close range froze Joe an instant before he could trigger off another round.

Not so Nimrod Jackson. The huge black man let go a roar and charged forward, firing his revolver wildly as he came . . . only to find himself flying heels-over-head through the air, watching a steaming water pot and the glowing coals of Tom's fire grow larger in his eyes until he fell face first into the embers. One hand lay in the heat-shimmering mass also, rendering it useless. Tanaka Tom stamped a calloused bare foot down on the elbow of Nimrod's gun arm in a *ka-sohu-tei*, depriving him of its use also. Then he turned his attention to Joe Coaker.

Joe fumbled his gun into position. Shoot low and you're bound to get him, his mind screamed. Joe fired, his mouth opening with awe-filled wonder as Tanaka Tom seemed to float into the air, straightening out except for one leg, cocked in a *tabi-geri*. As he neared Joe in seeming slow motion, he unleashed the stored power of the bent limb, driving it toward Joe's skull.

Blackness filled with pinpoints of brilliant light flooded the space behind Joe's eyes and he staggered sideways, dropping his six-gun. Tanaka Tom regained his feet, smashing into Joe's kidneys with two *yon hon nukite* spear thrust blows that drove the little gunslinger off balance, sending him crashing to the ground. Then Tom turned back to the screaming man in the fire.

Tanaka Tom rushed to Nimrod's side, reaching for his legs. The tea water had tipped over, extinguishing most of the glowing bed of coals, but in turn doing its

117

own fearsome damage to the big black's flesh. Tugging at Nimrod's pantlegs, Tom drew him clear of the heat. Then he rolled Nimrod onto his back.

Behind Tom, Joe Coaker shook a groggy head, fumbling to push himself upright. His left hand sought his hideout gun, fingers closing eagerly around the butt. He drew it swiftly and raised it to eye level, sighting at Tanaka Tom's broad back.

Chapter Fourteen

Head aching furiously, a fuzzy dimness at the edges of his vision, Joe Coaker tried to aim his revolver. He couldn't understand why there were now two men before him, clad in diaper-like loincloths. The muzzle wavered from one to the other. Biting his lip to hold back the pain he felt and to help him concentrate, Joe squeezed the trigger.

In the same instant, shrieking with the agony of his burned face, Nimrod Jackson sat up, hands clawing at his ruined flesh. Tanaka Tom stepped to the side, trying to restrain the man from further harming himself. As he did, Joe's gun blasted into the night. Joe's bullet caught Nimrod in his open, screaming mouth, ending forever the misery of his injuries. Nimrod flopped over backward and trembled slightly, then lay still. Swinging wide of the smoking gun in Joe's hand, Tom Fletcher closed in on him.

Sensing motion, Joe surged to his feet. He stood, swaying slightly, with the muzzle of the small revolver aimed carelessly between ground and sky. Tom swiftly moved in on the short outlaw. When he reached a distance of a couple of feet, Joe could see Tanaka Tom clearly and started to bring up his gun.

Tom delivered a rushing *mae geri keage* front kick to Joe's stomach. Coaker doubled over. His little, .32 caliber, swingout S&W revolver cracked sharply, sending a bullet past Tom's hip. Tom continued his move, closing and executing a bladehand *shuto* chop to the seventh vertebra at the base of Joe's neck. The bones of Joe's spine made a sound like a dry stick snapping and he pitched face first to the ground. He trembled violently a

119

few seconds, convulsed into a fetal position and lay still. Tom crossed the clearing, seized his *katana* and returned. He gave Joe the ritual stroke, severing his head from his corpse. As suddenly as it had begun, the violence ended.

"You proved to be a better man than the one you would avenge," Tom told the dead outlaw. Then he dragged the two bodies to a place among the rocks. Prying and digging with a stout shaft of manzanita, Tom dislodged enough dirt and rocks to cover them. Satisfied, he went in search of their horses. When he returned with them, he unsaddled the mounts, watered and hobbled them and settled down to sleep.

Sunrise found Tom Fletcher already up, brewing a pot of tea and boiling rice. As the white grains absorbed water, he stirred some slivers of dried fish—his last—into the glutinous mass. Leaving the cooking to its own course, Tom fed the horses and watered them again. All the while, he gave serious thought to a matter that had lain on his consciousness for some time.

In this country, given the ready availability of firearms, battle could be joined at a range far greater than possessed by sword or bow. He had soon observed, upon his arrival in the West, that any man who desired to carried one or more guns of varying types. Somehow, through a system of rather loose rules, this seemed to work. Yet, twenty years in a different culture argued to him that it threatened order and control.

For centuries, the common people of Japan, and certain religious orders, had been forbidden ownership of any form of weapons. Many among the tiny ruling class thought this to be the major factor that kept them in power. Hadn't karate, now an accepted martial art among the samurai, originated to protect the helpless from the excesses of their violence-prone overlords? In a land where everyone who wished to could go armed, such absolute power over life and death could not exist. Somewhere, his long-ago schoolboy memories pricked him, hadn't it been set down as a right of all the people? Whatever the case, experience had showed him that he must accomodate his tactics to fit this situation.

Ruefully, he recalled his clumsy, inexpert handling of the repeating rifle at the stagecoach robbery. Had the range not been so close, he might well have ended the loser in that contest. Not that Western arms were totally unknown in Japan. Cannon had been in use since the 1600s. Matchlock weapons had been brought in by the Portuguese. They had given way, in turn, to flintlock muskets and even percussion lock, rifled muskets of fairly recent manufacture. However, slaying indifferently and at such distance was still looked upon with scorn by the prideful samurai. They gloried in personal danger and close conflict. Where lay honor in killing a man at twice the range a bow could shoot? With such rhetorical questions they deprecated use of firearms. Official thinking, however, had differed on this since the coming of Perry.

Even before Tom departed for America, at the urging of the new emperor, a national army was being created. They would be organized, trained, and armed along the lines of the marines who accompanied the commodore to the islands. Outwardly, they were to be a defense force for use in the event of an invasion by the hordes of Chinese.

Privately, to his most trusted samurai, the ruler had confided that he saw in this army a means to swiftly put down any resistance to imperial authority and to eliminate once and for all any threat of the emergence of a rival faction to the power of the emperor. Most important of all, it would provide a means of expanding the empire. Thus, all things change and, since he now had access to arms and ammunition, it would be well to familiarize himself with their operation, Tom concluded.

His course for the day decided, Tom Fletcher went back to the fire and his first meal of the day. As his jaw methodically ground the food, he thought of how he would go about accomplishing his plan. He would begin with the rifles, having two to work with of different makes and caliber. Also he had past experience with muskets. His breakfast finished, he went to the saddles of the dead outlaws.

Nimrod Jackson had carried a Sharps repeating carbine. The heavy, .52 caliber piece felt slightly off balance to Tom, but he appreciated the smooth, comfortable way it lay against his cheek and sighted readily on a stunted manzanita shrub some sixty yards away. The large, brass, front sight blade lined up readily in the notch of the sliding leaf at the rear. Depressing the trigger guard loading lever with his knuckles, dropping the breech block, and allowing the magazine spring to feed into position one of the large, dull, red-brown, copper rim-fire cartridges made the gun ready to load. Closing the lever pushed the round into the chamber. The carrier block and breech pin made a smooth metallic sound as they went into place, shutting the breech and magazine. Tom jerked the trigger and nothing happened.

Checking carefully, he discovered that the side hammer functioned like that of a percussion lock. It had to be manually cocked each time. Earing it back, he sighted once more and applied force to the trigger. Forty-five grains of black powder detonated with the usual dull crash, shoving a 350 grain, .52 caliber bullet up the twenty-two-inch barrel at a respectable velocity of 970 feet per second. The eight-pound, four-ounce carbine slammed back into Tom's shoulder and the target was obscured by smoke.

When he could see again, Tom discovered that, like the first shot he'd fired during the stage robbery, he had hit low. A white scar marked the surface of a rock some two feet below the tree he'd aimed at. He reviewed what he had done. The sights, greatly improved over those of his previous experiences in Japan, should have made hitting simple. No, that couldn't be it. He actuated the lever again, ejecting the spent cartridge and chambering another of the seven rounds. He listened as he cocked the hammer. It lacked the accustomed rough, grating sound of older type weapons. Logic told him that a smoother action would require less pressure on the trigger. Yes! If he pulled too hard, it would cause the muzzle to jerk downward also. Once more he sighted on the scraggy manzanita.

This time, when the smoke drifted away, he saw a dark, raw earth gouge at the base of the tree. Even less pressure? He'd try it.

On the thirst attempt, a lower branch of the stringy, tough manzanita went flying away, split from the trunk by the huge conical lead bullet. Should he use an even lighter squeeze? He quickly chambered a fourth cartridge.

Stuck solidly, near the center of its trunk, the manzanita vibrated violently, stirring up a dust cloud. Even after the smoke cleared, a dull brown haze surrounded the small shrub. Elated, he rapidly expended the final three rounds, satisfied at his accomplishment. Tanaka Tom set the carbine aside and picked up Joe Coaker's Winchester "Yellow Boy."

It was a model 1866, an improvement on the Henry patent, with bronze side and base plates for the receiver, and blued, round, twenty-inch barrel and magazine tube. Its seven-pound, twelve-ounce weight felt more functional in his hands and the straight stock comb let it throw up into sighting position easily. He actuated the cocking lever, noticing how the block rode backward, rather than dropping, cocking the hammer in the process. Closing it, he chambered a copper, .44 caliber, rim-fire cartridge. He took aim and fired. Tom hardly felt the recoil as the steel butt plate pushed against his shoulder, driven by a lighter, 28 grain powder charge. Surprise registered on his face when he saw a small branch clipped away by the 200 grain conical bullet. Moving at 1,125 feet per second, it had reached the target before smoke from the muzzle blossomed large enough to obscure the view. He fired again.

By the time Tom had exhausted the Winchester's twelve round capacity, he felt comfortable with it and confident of his ability. He set it aside, for including in his own assortment of weapons. Now he would investigate the mysteries of the handguns.

First he examined the Smith and Wesson No. 2,

army model, .32 hideout gun Coaker had tried to kill him with the previous night. Comparing its puny cartridge with those of the Sharps and Winchester and noticing the crude, hacksaw job of shortening the barrel, he discarded it as not sufficiently functional. Later, he decided, he might fire it for practice. Next, he examined Nimrod Jackson's converted Remington. It was a factory conversion job, complete with extractor, although Tom was not aware of this or its importance. Holding it at waist height, as he had seen the black man do, he fired one round at the tree, managing only to startle a flight of birds. He tried again, with equally poor results. He'd have to change his style.

Extending his arm to full length, sighting this time, he shot a third round. The bullet sang a high-pitched scream as it ricocheted off a rock face some three feet to the right of the manzanita. All right, he'd try two hands.

This attempt gained better results. He hit the target, though not where he'd aimed. Quickly he fired the fifth cartridge. He noted little improvement. Then the hammer fell on an empty cylinder. Puzzled as to why a man would carry only five rounds in a six-shooter, he examined the piece. He had the answer in a second. The long, fine point of the firing pin extended well into the space between cylinder and back plate. If all six chambers were loaded it could result in an accidental discharge. Now to try again.

A few moments' careful experimentation showed Tom the purpose of the extractor rod and he reloaded the gun. Five more rounds convinced him that the revolver had not been designed for as fine accuracy as a carbine or rifle. He sat it aside, though keeping it in mind—at least it fired the same ammunition as the Winchester carbine. He picked up Coaker's Colt, an 1872 model Frontier revolver in .44 rim-fire.

First off he noted a smoothness in the action, lacking in the cap and ball conversion Remington. The workmanship and finishing of parts seemed superior, too, as though the earlier model had been turned out rapidly, in great quantities, with little care or attention given to eliminating rough spots. Of course, this had been the case; the Remington was made under contract for the Union Army during the Civil War. The lines, including those of the fluted chamber, and balance appealed to him also. He took aim, one handed and, on only the second shot, had the satisfaction of watching a limb fly from the manzanita. Pleased, he fired the cylinder empty and reloaded.

Tom pumped four more cylinders full through the Colt, gaining in ability and appreciation all the while. He stopped at last and sat in the shade of a large boulder, thinking over an idea that had slowly grown in his mind. Noon came and passed, yet he took no time for a meal. The more thought he gave it, the more convinced he became it would work. What would happen, he asked himself, if he applied the principles of karate and the techniques of *kyūjutsu* archery to pistol and rifle shooting? He could see no way it might possibly produce worse results. Excited, he loaded all the firearms again.

Taking three quick, deep breaths and concentrating his mental power—something that had become second nature to him over the past twenty years—Tom brought mind and body into one being, focused through his *ki* force. Eyes fixed on the distant target, he reached out in what seemed a casual manner and picked up the Spencer carbine. He held it part-way between hip and shoulder, arm partially extended. Projecting his consciousness of future actions as he willed them to be through the gun barrel, across space, and into the heart of his mark, he eared back the hammer and squeezed off a round.

A small square of white cloth he had attached to the manzanita suddenly grew a black hole in the lower left corner. He worked the action and fired again. Another hit. Keeping his rhythm smooth, motions uniform, mental force tightly centered, he emptied the seven-shot magazine. When the last smoke blew from the target, the three-inch patch of fabric could absorb not another puncture. Maintaining the outward placid composure of perfect *ki*, while inwardly exulting, Tanaka Tom replaced his target with a second piece of material, set the Spencer aside, and took up the Winchester.

Twelve rounds later, an irregular, sideward leaning figure eight had been chewed out of the right-center of the cloth. Now came the great challenge, the six-guns. Tom chose the Remington first. With a new target in place, he took careful aim to get a starting point.

The first round struck low and right, clipping the edge of the white patch. Now, shooting from the same position, between hip and shoulder, he proceeded to fire two cylinder loads. Extending onto the wood of the manzanita trunk, a roughly egg-shaped pattern had been produced, the small end downward. It could be covered, he estimated, with a small saucer. Next came the real test, with the Colt.

Tom's grouping was tighter, entirely on the white target, slightly right of center, leaving only small shreds in the four corners. Allowing his satisfaction to show at last, Tom reloaded the Colt, then filled the empty cartridge loops in the pistol belt from a box he took from Coaker's saddle bags. Then he loaded the Winchester and placed it in its scabbard, which he attached to his saddle. Next, he stowed the remaining firearms in his pack, along with all the ammunition available. The time had come, he figured, now that he had the skill needed, to take on the massive firepower of Hollister's gang in Ajo. Tom wasted no time in making ready to leave.

Chapter Fifteen

Huge dark shapes, long scrawny necks extended, seemed to hang motionless in the air on widespread wings. Tom Fletcher observed them for several miles as he rode toward the small town of Ajo. They maintained their circular vigil by nearly imperceptible movements of their great black and white pinions. A little over a mile from the Hayes ranch, where he had stopped to care for his wound, he began to notice the smell.

Sharpest of the odors came from the acrid essence of burned wood, mixed with the pungent tang of smoke that still rose from several closely spaced places. Overlaying other scents, though, he could perceive the sickly sweet redolence of death. Worried by this, Tom applied heels to his Morgan, stretching out the string of animals he led.

Fire-scarred trees first came into view, the leaves still green, but withered and sere. Then, as though a circle had been drawn from top to bottom, a little past the trunk of the cottonwoods, their foliage changed to dry, fluttering, colorless bits, growing shriveled and darker brown as they neared the side once closest to the house. Finally, only naked, charred and blackened branches remained. Where the house once stood, a white ash-covered mound of coals glowed dully and pulsated with trapped heat.

In the midst of this desolation, Tanaka Tom reined in, quieting his nervous animals. The barn had likewise been burnt to the ground, along with all the other outbuildings. Looking around, Tom located the source of attraction for the vultures wheeling in the sky above him, content to wait their turn.

Little Tory Hayes had been hacked and slashed and shot at least twice. His healthy young child's body had fought valiantly to retain life. Emmy, his sister, had not died easily either. Tom dismounted and walked to where the girl lay. Her torn clothes did little to cover her nakedness and he could see that she had been badly used by several men, in a number of ways, before death mercifully ended her ordeal. Unbidden, Tom Fletcher's mind superimposed these images upon what must have happened at his family's plantation eight years before. Flames of anger flared up within him and his lips peeled back in a feral grimace of hatred. He turned away, nearly stumbling over the rancher's body.

Ben Hayes lay near his daughter. The look of horror and revulsion, frozen on his face by death, indicated that he had been forced to witness Emmy's degradation before a bullet in the back of his head ended his life. Their only crime had been to aid him, Tom thought bitterly, and to stand in the way of Pike Turner and his men. Another score, added to his own, to settle with Colonel Edward Hollister and those who rode for him, Tanaka Tom promised himself. He walked away, looking for a shovel that might have survived the fire. At least he could give these people a decent burial. The rumble of many hoofs, rapidly approaching the ranch-yard, interrupted his search. His hand went to his *katana*, fingers closing on the grip, partially drawing it from the scabbard.

Suddenly Tom found himself surrounded by twelve drawn guns. Grim-faced, sun-browned men sat their lathered horses, cold eyes flashing hate at the stranger they had cornered. One man, his hair shot with gray, apparently the leader, pushed back the brim of his Stetson. The muzzle of the Sharps in his other hand never wavered from Tom's chest.

"Well, now appears we caught one of them already, boys." To Tom he snapped angrily, "You figure to rob the dead, you son of a bitch?"

"You are right in one thing. I caused their deaths, though not in the way you think. The men you seek are in Ajo. They came here hunting me. Ben Hayes dressed

128

a wound for me, one I received in a fight with Pike Turner's outlaws. When word came that searchers were out, Ben Hayes suggested it would be safer for me if I moved on, took refuge at the hidden spring not far from here."

As though he had not heard a word Tom said, the graying man turned his seamed face to a young cowboy. "Lorry, you found them. Told me they was hacked up with a hatchet or something like it. Could it have been that . . . thing he's got his hand on?"

Tom's chest swelled with confidence and pride. "My *katana* can slice a man cleanly in half lengthwise—two and a half men, according to the inscription on the tang—with only moderate force behind the stroke. You, who are so anxious to use the rope . . . step down and I'll gladly show you. Look at the way the bodies are torn, the bones smashed. The blade that did that is a crude one, poorly made. A fieldhand's knife. I killed the Negro who used it. Him and another man named Joe Coaker. They're buried back at the spring."

One of the riders kneed his horse forward. "He's got somethin' there, Mr. Barton. Them fellers we came across early yesterday were all strangers. They wouldn't know about the spring, 'less someone told them. An' they had a big buck with 'em."

"He's right, Mr. Barton," another cowboy added. "And I'm sure none of them rode a Morgan."

"Tied to my saddlehorn is a cloth bag," Tom casually informed his stern inquisitor. "It contains a token I intended to give to Pike Turner . . . before I killed him. I think it will prove what I said about myself and my sword."

"Go get it," Abe Barton commanded. He shifted in his saddle, easing legs tired by age more than distance. His black, glowering stare returned to Tom Fletcher.

A bandy-legged puncher reined his horse to the left and rode to where Tom had tied his Morgan to one of the fire-blackened cottonwoods. He leaned forward in the saddle and untied a heavy, rounded sack, carrying it back to Abe Barton with a crinkle-faced look that betrayed his offended nostrils.

"Pheew! Whatever it is, Mr. Barton, it sure as hell stinks."

Impatiently, Barton jerked open the drawstring and plunged one big, weather-reddened hand into the opening. His face took on a look of uncomfortable surprise, tinged with a touch of sickened fear that the contents might indeed be what he had begun to suspect they might be. Without any noticeable hesitation, though, he jerked the cloth free of its burden. The two cowboys closest to their boss gagged, making croaking, choking noises and leaned far over the side of their mounts to vomit.

Joe Coaker's glazed eyes stared sightlessly back at them, mouth open in distorted anguish, the flesh of his severed head discolored, purplish tongue lolling. Clear for all to see, the point where it had been cut from his neck was as smooth and neat as though done by a surgeon's knife. Several more men shied their horses backward a few steps to avoid the sight.

Even the plowshare-hard Abe Barton felt his stomach give a warning lurch. "Where . . . what . . . why did you do this?"

"It is the custom where I come from."

"Where is that?"

"Japan. There are two reasons for decapitation. The first is to honor a friend who has taken *seppuku-do*, the way of self-destruction to right a wrong, or of an enemy who has fought well and honorably. In this manner it insures he shall be reborn as a samurai. The second purpose is to give warning to an implacable foe that no quarter shall be given. Such as one would to bandits. Look about you.

"What you see is the work of marauders or bandits. Having nothing themselves, they have no respect for that which belongs to others. They exist only to loot and destroy, taking a fiendish delight in the horror they create in the minds of those who witness their deeds. Such are the scum who did this. They are led by a man named Pike Turner, an underling of Colonel Edward Hollister. When you came upon me, I was preparing to bury these friends who died for helping me.

130

"Then I was going to Ajo to serve notice on Pike Turner that one at a time or in groups, I would kill every man with him. That accounts for the head. Now, as to my own unworthy person.

"In my adopted country—yes, I am an American, as much so by birth as you, though I've spent twenty years in Japan—I am in personal service to the former shogun, once the temporal head of the government, who was in turn answerable to the emperor. As such, I rank as a daimyo of the fourth class, sort of a lesser lord by European standards. By American criteria, I am wealthy beyond the needs of two lifetimes. Therefore, I have no necessity to rob or steal or loot to make a living. In the way of *bushido*, the warrior code of Japan, a blood feud exists between Hollister and myself. I seek vengeance, for what was done to my family, against Hollister and all the men who served under him. Pike Turner is one of those men. There is nothing further I can tell you."

Tom Fletcher stood with bowed head. He seemed resigned to accept whatever might befall him. His true state, however differed greatly from his outward appearance. His eyes busily gathered information for his mind, active in deciding where to strike first, second, and on until he won or lost, should these men's decision go against him. He maintained this pose even when Abe Barton gruffly cleared his throat.

"Well, damnit, men, get some shovels and let's help bury these folks. It's the least we can do for a neighbor. Then, sir, if you will have us along, we'll join you in your fight against this Turner."

"My name is Fletcher, Tom Fletcher. I thank you for your offer of assistance." Tom looked up into Barton's eyes, sparkling now with friendly interest. "About going with me to Ajo. I am not sure that would be a good idea. There are some things . . ." he nodded toward the head, still held, neglected, by Barton ". . . that I am honor bound to do which you may find distasteful . . . objectionable."

"By God, Fletcher . . . ah, Tom, the Hayes family were neighbors to me. I watched those kids grow from babies, helped Ben dig his wife's grave. Any man here

131

that hasn't stomach to do this thing your way, why they can light a shuck right now."

"That goes for me, too," the young cowboy with lynch fever announced forcefully.

"Good boy, Brad. I knew we could count on you." To Tom, Barton explained, "Brad here's a reliable hand and a good man to back you in a brawl. Long as he knows whose side who is on, he'll stand by you."

"You have struck upon only one of many problems connected with my having assistance. Let me . . . think on it a moment, eh?"

"Certainly, certainly." Barton, relaxed and affable now, went to join his ranch hands in digging graves. Two men remained behind, dismounting.

"Ah . . . er, we're Mr. Hayes's hands. Anyway, we were. I'm the one . . . found them. What you say sounds right enough, mister. And I suppose you got good enough call to go after this Hollister by yerself. But Ben Hayes was good to me. He gave me a home when I had none, took me in when I was on'y fourteen and skirtin' the edge of the owlhoot trail. He made a man of me and treated me like one of his own. Now you got ever' right to get revenge for your family, like you tell. I figger the same goes for me.

"You can tell the others they can't go along if you want. Nothin' you say, though, can stop me from goin' after the men who killed the only family I ever had."

For a long while the two men stood looking at each other, Tom deep in contemplation, Lorry Garnett bristling with his challenge. After a few seconds, Tom broke off the eye-to-eye confrontation. A small hint of a smile played around his firm mouth.

"Barton-*san* called you Lorry, is that it?"

"Yes, sir. Lorry Garnett."

Tom gestured toward where preparations were being conducted for the burial. "You have given me yet another thing to consider, Lorry. For the others, the original question remains. Why would they risk death or injury for the honor of a family already cold and in the ground? Why fight at all, for that matter?"

"I suppose it's because out here we got somethin' like

132

that 'bushy doe' you were talking about. Ever'body's got to be willin' to stand alongside his neighbor against Injuns, outlaws, whatever comes, or we get picked off one by one."

Tom's smile bloomed fully now. "*Bushido*, you mean? Yes, I see your point. Which only leaves my personal conflict at issue. Do I want any help? This is a matter of honor for me. Can I satisfy the demands of honor, can I keep face, if I ask others to risk their lives for my cause? Or do I lose face if others succeed where I fail to the extent I must recover honor only through the way of *seppuku*?"

Lorry's face washed blank with disbelief. "You mean you'd kill yourself if we got them jaspers instead of you?"

"Certainly. I would have no other choice." He nodded toward where the graves were being dug. "But come, let us go pay honor to a worthy man and those he loved. It will give me more time to make a decision."

An hour later, the men sat astride their horses in the ruined ranchyard. In a swirl of dust, Tanaka Tom pulled his Morgan out in front of Abe Barton and his cowhands. He drew his *katana* and waved it high above his head. In an instant quiet held over the group.

"Pike Turner is the enemy. All of you have sworn to revenge these killings upon him and his men. So be it. That is his karma . . . and yours. Yet you wish to ride with me to do it." A grim smile slashed his face for a moment and he hefted the cotton cloth bag with its gruesome trophy. "My ways of fighting are not yours. Know this, though. If you ride with me, you take orders from me. We will fight in the place and the manner I decide."

A grumble of objection rose among the cowboys as they looked at each other, unsure of where they stood. Tom hurried on with his explanation.

"I know that Barton-*san* is your boss, the man you take orders from. But in this you will obey me or you will not ride with us. Any who cannot abide by this

133

should leave now." Having spoken his decision, Tom Fletcher waited quietly, calmly.

The cowmen shifted uneasily, each hesitant to be the first to commit himself. Then Lorry Garnett nudged his horse forward, riding out to swing into line beside Tanaka Tom.

"Count me in."

Abe Barton came forward next. He reined up on Tom's other side. His granite jaw and steely eyes swept over his men. "Well? What the hell are you randies waiting for?"

With an exuberant shout the cowboys jumped their ponies forward, swirling around the three motionless riders at the center of their snorting, dust-roiling mass. For the first time that day, Tom Fletcher grinned sincerely, a feeling of warmth and comradeship spreading through him. He hefted his sword again, sunlight striking bright shafts from its raw steel blade.

"*Banzai! Banzai*! We ride to Ajo!"

Twilight lingered redly on the western horizon as Tanaka Tom's small army waited behind a ridge overlooking Ajo. The thudding sounds of a single horse's hoofs came clearly to them in the quiet desert air. In a few minutes Abe Barton rode over the crest. He swung wide of the trail and reined up in front of Tom Fletcher. Tom had selected the rancher as the least-likely to arouse suspicion when he rode into the small town and also as most likely to obtain the needed information and make a cogent report.

"What news?"

Barton scowled. "Damn bad news if you ask me."

"What do you mean? Has Turner been reinforced?"

"No. At least not that I know of. Folks I talked to said only one man joined them. A fancy dressed, dude sort. Turner and the others called him, 'Colonel.' Looks like it might be the feller you're lookin' for. Anyway, what's bad is this. They all pulled out. Lock, stock and barrel, takin' wagons loaded with loot. Anything that weren't nailed down from the way the townsfolk tell it. Been gone since about noon. Worst luck, they're headed south. I cut their trail outside town. Wagon ruts as deep as the old prairie schooners."

"What makes it so bad that they are headed south?"

Barton looked at Tom, startled by his questioning of the obvious. "Mexico. Once they cross that border, if they've got the money to back them up, they're as safe as if they were a million miles away."

Tom didn't hesitate an instant before replying to Barton. "Then the solution is for us to catch them before they get there. Let's ride."

Chapter Sixteen

Even as darkness had forced an end to pursuit, so had the night halted Edward Hollister and his men. By hard, fast travel, pushing their horses to the point of blowing them, Tom Fletcher and his small force had closed the gap that separated them from the slow-moving wagons. The two camps, though neither was aware of the other at first, were less than a mile apart. A huge bonfire, built by the men under Pike Turner's command, alerted Tanaka Tom to the proximity of his enemy.

Seated near the blaze, Edward Hollister leaned back against a wagon wheel, a saddle blanket padding the hard oaken spokes. He took from his pocket several folded sheets of paper, listing the items "confiscated" from Ajo.

Opening them, he began going over the array, a soaring sense of satisfaction filling his chest. Sawed lumber, enough to build two large mansions; nails, hardware, fixtures and sacks of mortar; everything needed to finish those buildings. Panes of glass, carefully crated, Pike had assured him, mirrors, fancy chandeliers, rifles—fifty of them—ammunition, revolvers, cases of explosives, paint, kerosene, liquor, flour, beans, sugar, coffee, tea, horseshoes, nails, round and bar stock, an anvil and forge, bellows . . . my God, the list seemed endless, he thought with a start. And money! A bit over eleven thousand dollars in gold coin and paper currency. He could outfit and support a small army with the loot take from Ajo. His full, sensual lips formed a satisfied smile as his mind recalled Edmond's lines from *King Lear*.

136

"I grow . . . I prosper . . . Now, gods, stand up for bastards!"

"More coffee, colonel?"

Edward Hollister looked up to see Pike Turner standing over him, a steaming granite pot in his hand. "Uh . . . yes, Captain Turner. Thank you. I will. And, ah . . . Pike, when you've done with that, come back. We have a lot to talk over."

"Yes, sir. I'll do that."

When Pike Turner returned, he found his boss in a reflective mood. Liquor passed freely among the men and a party-like atmosphere prevailed in the camp. Edward Hollister seemed not to notice it, however. His eyes, distant and clouded, focused on some other place or time, and a bemused smile quirked up the corners of his mouth. Pike sat down, spoke diffidently.

"You wanted to discuss something with me, Colonel?"

"When I was a child, we had things pretty rough, Pike. My father had just brought us out from Boston to Ohio. His business was new, there were few people settled that far west at the time. For several years we ate biscuits and red-eye gravy, with occasional bacon rinds, for our only meal of the day. Oh, there weren't many who were better off than us in the Ohio Valley, but the memory of going to bed hungry and waking even hungrier and spending the day with a gnawing, empty sensation in my belly has stayed with me. Did you know I can't stand the thought of being short on food? Even when my larder is full to overflowing, I seem compelled to acquire more and more. The fear of going hungry haunts me.

"Things got better, of course. Back in fifty, fifty-one, during the prosperity that came on the coattails of the gold rush to California, my father made quite a fortune. I was in my late teens then. Suddenly, it seemed like overnight, we were rich. Ah, the social invitations, the parties, the girls who flocked around. The plans I made, the dreams I had. Cincinnati was a large city by that time. Prosperity seemed to be there for good. Then I learned the awful truth. Something that, young and

137

unworldly as I was, seemed to shatter all my dreams, destroy my hopes for the future." Pike Turner made no reply, so Hollister continued.

"I learned, quite by accident, that the man I knew as my father was not my blood parent. I had come across some letters, some old papers, a journal kept by my mother. From that diary, I discovered that I had been nearly a year old when Mother married Melville Hollister."

"She had been married before?" Pike Turner suggested.

"No. My fahter, though she never identified him by name in her journal, had been a 'seafaring man,' an officer on a foreign ship, with a roguish way and a beguiling tongue. He and my mother were lovers for several months. Then, when she discovered she had become pregnant, and told him, he signed papers on the first available ship and sailed out of Boston, never to return. Eighteen months later, she met and married Melville Hollister. I took his name and the move West broke all ties with the truth. Thought nothing could change the fact that bastard I had been born and bastard I remained.

"My newfound friends in high society knew nothing of it, of course. Yet, I constantly tormented myself with the fear that they would discover it. If I did, surely they could, too. I got to feeling as though they could tell by looking at me, as though illegitimacy somehow branded a person with some visible stigma. I began to avoid social gatherings, withdrawing into myself. My pursuits became sedentary and intellectual. By the time I reached maturity I had the reputation of being an eccentric. Then my father . . . uh, Melville Hollister died. He left everything to me, except his grand home on Chandler in Cincinnati. That, and a large annuity, Mother received."

Unseen by the talking man, first one, then several other of the men stopped what they were doing and gathered around. Soon Hollister had a quiet, expectant audience as he went on with his reminiscences.

"When the war came along, I saw in it my chance for

fulfillment. I would organize a regiment, finance them entirely from my fortune and ride off to battle. I should either die valorously or live to claim honor and glory. Whichever way, or so I thought, it would erase the stain of my bastardy." He seemed to notice his audience for the first time. "There, in the regiment, is where so many of us first met. You, Pike, were the best company commander I had. You knew more about war and tactics than I did. Like so many others in that conflict, my money took the place of experience. Though I had no past soldiering, I bought my commission as colonel by providing my own regiment to command. My God, when I think back on it, it's a wonder any of us lived through that holocaust. The Rebels had trained, professional officers, they had soldiers who had fought the Mexicans, Indians, some who had hired out to foreign countries. We were, compared to them, like a lot of small boys setting out to play at war with those brightly painted lead soldiers from Vienna and Berlin.

"Yes, it was men like you, Pike . . . and you, Ace, and other fine officers I had that brought us through. There was Brad Cone, Ashton, even our sutler, Jeffrey Nash, all loyal then and even now. Except for Ashton. He always was a queer duck. Last I heard he had been touched by religious mania. No doubt losing his father and two brothers in the short span of one winter unhinged his reason. I went to him at the time, offered once more for him to share our destiny. He refused."

"Better off without him," Pike Turner opined. "He made my skin crawl. Don't forget the noncommissioned officers and the rank-and-file."

"How could I? Harry Kitchner was the very model of a perfect sergeant major. A born organizer. Cool under fire and positively inventive in finding ways of learning where those Rebel sluts had hidden the silver plates." The men around him laughed heartily. "Paxton and Porter . . . inseparable friends since boyhood. They have a detachment of their own now. They are engaged in preparing things in the Northwest. It did my heart good to promote them to commissioned rank. They richly deserved it. Remember how they covered for us

139

while we visited those plantations along the Savannah?"

Shouts of laughter rose again as men carried their thoughts back with their colonel to those bygone days of looting and lust. They exchanged reminiscences, vying with one another to recall a favored anecdote. Their noisy chatter went on for over half an hour. Only C. C. Steel remained quiet, reliving his own memories, sharing them with no one.

Mention of the Savannah River had brought to his mind vivid recollections of one particular young boy. A towhead of eleven, maybe twelve years. It was a small plantation. What was the name? Flickenger? Farnsworth? Fowler . . . never mind, the name wasn't important now. A most satisfying encounter. Too bad, he thought with regret, that the colonel had lopped off the little lad's head during a fit of drunken rage. The plans he'd had for the child. Take him along for a while. Educate him to the finer points of . . . of . . . but never mind. All that was past now.

"Yes, sir, those were the days!" The colonel's words brought an end to their retrospection. "We've some even better ones coming. Mexico, boys, just think of it! From what I hear, they are rife with discontent, poverty, and revolution. Why, within a year, I wouldn't be surprised if we were to have our own country from which to base our conquest of the West. We'll move cautiously at first. But when our hour comes . . . Oh, what a fine time we'll have!"

Confiding only in Abe Barton, Tom Fletcher slipped out of camp to scout the enemy. He moved effortlessly, so quietly that he didn't even disturb the sleeping birds, as he closed in on the high bluff where the wagons were gathered in a large circle, tongue to tail. A huge, blinding fire blazed in the center of the open space within their confines. Men laughed and talked loudly, passing bottles of whiskey around, drinking deeply. No effort, Tom was surprised to find, had been made to place a guard. At first he found no one he could identify, then Pike Turner appeared at the fire, picking up a pot of coffee.

140

Tom watched him across the circle to a a place where a man sat against a wagon wheel. Like Turner, he wore a better cut of clothes than most of the men and the deference shown him by Turner convinced Tom that this was Edward Hollister. Tom was too far away to hear clearly when Hollister began talking. As time passed and the men arranged themselves in a silent cluster around their leader, Tom was able to work his way closer.

He clearly heard Hollister's reference to the plantations on the Savannah River and his anger flared from a low glow of coals to white-hot fury. When the men took up their own accounts of those raids, one of which had surely been the Fletcher place, Tom realized that nearly everyone present had taken part in the despoiling and murder of his family. Here rested a chance to gain revenge on practically every man on his list. To strike at Hollister himself as well. Beside himself with anticipation, Tom made careful mental note of the layout of the outlaw camp and slipped quietly away into the darkness.

Back with the small posse of cowboys, he called them together and started laying out his plans for battle. They would attack at sunrise, he informed them.

Chapter Seventeen

"What the hell's he puttin' on?" the cowboy's whispered question broke through the damp chill of pre-dawn.

"Looks like some sort of armor to me," Abe Barton replied, wishing silently for a good, hot cup of coffee.

"That's what it is," Lorry Garnett informed them. "We talked about it earlier. It's what these, ah, samurai wear into battle."

Tanaka Tom Fletcher had exchanged his Levi's for the padded, baggy trousers and greaves of samurai battle armor and slipped into the quilted, knee-length, flare-skirted *gi* worn under his breastplate. He quickly struggled into the leather-strap-hinged corselet, which consisted of back- and breast-plates. The latter was made of overlapping layers of saltwater-hardened leather with plates of fire-hardened wood and bone riveted to them. Next he attached the broad, armored epaulets that protected his collarbone and the vulnerble shoulder joints and base of his neck. Tom reached into the leather envelope, his parfleche, and took out his mask and donned it.

"You're the expert, Lorry. What's he wearin' a mask for?" the cowboy inquired again.

"It's to frighten his enemies, Stan."

"I can see how it would do that. God, it's ugly."

Ready but for his over-large, flare-bottomed, scuttle-shaped helmet, which he slung by its chin strap on his left forearm, Tom turned to the others, signaling them to gather around.

"As I told you last night, we can't ride up on them. They'd hear our horses coming and be able to make a break for it."

Grumbles rose among the men. There wasn't a one of them who, if he could straddle a horse, would not prefer to ride half a block rather than walk. Tom let their complaints die down before continuing.

"If we pad our horses' hoofs with rags, we can walk them, mounted, to within a quarter mile or so. From there we make it on foot. That's the reason we're starting so early.

"When we get there, be careful moving through the rocks. Don't make a sound. As much as they were drinking last night, there probably won't be anyone on guard, or sober if they are. Likely we can catch them all asleep. We'll surround the camp as best we can with the men we have. No one fires a shot until I give the signal. You all understand?" Silence greeted his question. "All right, then. Let's move out and no talking or smoking by anyone from now on."

Willie Oelicher, formerly a private and headquarters orderly, 251st Ohio, awoke with a throbbing head. He knew he should stick to beer. But, he thought, with so much likker floatin' around, what could a feller be expected to do? His eyes felt as though they had been rubbed in sand, his tongue was dry and swollen, and a foul odor emanated from his mouth like something escaped from a crypt. He sat up—he was supposed to have been on lookout—and the effort nearly knocked him back again. Rocks and trees around the bluff, things ordinarily solid and substantial, began quavering and undulating around. A sharp pain in his kidneys and the insistent pressure of his bladder brought a moan to Willie's lips. Unsteadily, he got to his feet.

One hand to his pulsating head, the other to the small of his back, he wobbled on unsupportive legs to a spot among the rocks.

"Gotta take a leak . . . gotta go leak," he croaked repeatedly as though to remind himself of the purpose of his venture.

Reaching a sheltered spot, his fingers fumbled at his fly a few moments and then he began to make water. A sudden surge of nausea doubled him over and he spewed out the sour, liquor-scented contents of his unstable stomach. When the spasm passed, he stood upright and froze, eyes bugging in horror, mouth agape.

"Oh, God! So help me, Jesus, I'll never touch another drop again. I swear it, God. D-d-don't let it get me!"

There, before Willie's protuberant eyes, seeming to rise out of the very rock, came a demon right out of hell. That or one of those things a feller was supposed to see when he'd hit the bottle too much. Not an overly religious man, Willie preferred to believe the latter, although compelled to give consideration to the former possibility. That accounted for the oath to foreswear hard liquor that he grunted out in a coarse whisper a second before he died.

Tanaka Tom Fletcher crouched low among the rocks at the edge of the bluff where Hollister's men camped. He watched as the slumbering sentry awakened and rose, walking Tom's way. He saw the man stop, begin to relieve himself and then bend low to vomit up the remains of his previous night's celebration. As wave after wave of sickness welled up in the man, Tom surged to his feet, his *katana* high over his head. When the guard straightened and looked up, Tanaka Tom was ready to make his stroke.

Willie Oelicher died without making a sound after his hurried prayer. The samurai sword whistled through the air and bit into his flesh at the base of Willie's neck, cleaving through his collarbone, ribs, and spine, slicing him open to the navel. Tanaka Tom withdrew his blade and Willie's body fell away. He jumped onto a rock closer to the camp, in sight of everyone, waving his blood-drenched *katana* above his head. There he yelled his defiance to the outlaws below him.

"Edward Hollister! Come out, Edward Hollister, and fight me. Murderer of women and children, man of no honor, coward, come forth and fight one against one . . . or all here shall die!

"I am Tanaka Ichimara Tomi of the *Fujika rentai*, Master of Horse and Standard Bearer to the shogun. I

144

am the first into battle and the last to leave the field. I have killed thirty-one men, three of whom were Frank Tollar, Joe Coaker, and a Negro whose name I do not know. I now claim as mine the lives of Edward Hollister, Pike Turner, and many of the men who ride with them. Like the mighty Divine Wind, the *kamakazi*, I bring death and destruction. Show yourselves and prepare to die!"

Life stirred in the camp. Men, groaning with their hangovers, reached for guns with one hand and their boots with the other. A shot blasted at the black silhouette standing on the rocks with the rising sun behind him. Tom quickly whirled away, slashing downward with his great sword. As he disappeared from view, he gave a loud cry.

"Now!"

A ring of smoke seemed to envelope the rocks circling the small bluff. Bullets plowed into the dirt. A man cried out, clutching his arm, his weapon and clothes forgotten. Another man, dashing toward the protecting ring of wagons, stumbled, falling onto his chest. His legs churned a few seconds and grew still. C. C. Steel bleated in a shrill, effeminate voice and sought protection in a wagon box. His mind churned with grief over the loss of Nimrod Jackson—whom he considered to be sweet and gentle, the only one of Hollister's rowdy gang who truly understood him—and fear for his own life as he watched the battle's progress.

Two outlaws dashed to the picketline and freed their horses. Mounting, they tried to break out of the encircling death. They no sooner jumped a wagon tongue and hurtled among the rocks than the incredible looking figure of Tanaka Tom loomed up between them.

Tom held a smoking Colt Frontier in his left hand, his *katana* in the right. The whistling blade made a streak of orange light in the rising sun as it flashed toward one rider. The escaping gunman, a former corporal in the 251st Ohio, never saw the blade. His momentum nearly wrenched the sword from Tom's hand, but it sliced cleanly through ribs and collarbone, separating a large portion of the right side of the bandit's chest from the rest of his body. In the same instant, Tanaka Tom eared back the hammer of the .44 rim-fire revolver and snapped off a shot at the dying gunslinger's companion.

Striking under the left armpit, the big 215 grain, conical, lead bullet pulped lung tissue, nicked the top lobe of the heart and ripped a wide tear in the aorta before altering direction and plowing out of the man's back, bringing a rib root and a portion of spinal column with it. As though snatched away by a rope, the rider left the frightened horse's bare back. The animal whinnied in panic and charged off down the loose slope to the desert below. Tanaka Tom ducked from sight. Somewhere in the dusty, milling confusion inside the ring of wagons, a bugle sounded recall.

Edward Hollister couldn't believe what happened around him. How could they have been so cleverly ambushed? A steady hail of lead buzzed angrily through the small circle inside the drawn-up wagons. Dust rose and men screamed and died. Most of all he felt confusion and, far back in his mind, an aching dread. Who was this man with the strange-sounding name? Why did he want to kill him? In the fury of battle Hollister had no time to ponder his own questions or give answers. He saw his two escaping troopers cut down by the big man in the outlandish outfit. Amazing. It appeared as though he had no need of looking directly at a target he engaged, yet he didn't miss with either gun or sword. That sword. Where had he seen one like it before? At least that was something he could understand and deal with. He located his sabre and made ready. The next time this Tanaka Whatchamacallit showed his face, he'd move in on him.

Sheldon Voss had had enough. He couldn't take any more of this sitting down to die. If he could get behind whoever was out there, he could catch them in a cross fire. That should give a couple of others a chance to do the same. He heard the bugle sound recall and ignored it while he waited his chance, then made a break for it.

146

Only a single bullet spanged off rock near Sheldon's hip as he dashed in among the rocks. On knees and elbows he wormed his way through to a position from which the attackers could not see him. He stood to come face to face with the hideous, snarling, painted-on features of Tanaka Tom's battle mask. Voss's mouth fell open as he took in the simulated rage, bulging eyes, and black strands of hair that made up a drooping mustache that swayed listlessly in the light breeze. Seemingly compelled by a force outside him, he let go of his Spencer carbine and it clattered to the ground.

"What is your name?"

Caught unawares by the unexpected question, Sheldon Voss stammered an answer. "Voss. Sheldon Voss. Why?"

The grotesque features of the mask seemed to acquire life of their own. The helmeted head nodded. "You're on the list. Remember the Fletcher plantation? A man, his wife, a little girl, a boy about twelve? A place on the Savannah River?"

Sheldon Voss swallowed hard. He nodded, afraid to trust his own voice. The huge figure facing him raised his arm while the sword glided into position. Voss felt mesmerized. Again the frightful apparition spoke.

"I am Tom Fletcher. This is for my family."

At first, Voss thought Fletcher had missed. The sword whistled through the air, he felt a short, sharp pain, but nothing else seemed to happen. Then his body folded slackly from under his severed head, which also fell to the ground, rolling over so that the sightless eyes gaped at the sky. Tanaka Tom started off through the rocks.

Rounding a boulder he came onto Edward Hollister. Despite the obscuring mask, Tanaka Tom's elation and anticipation could clearly be understood. Giving a sharp cry, he leaped forward, *katana* flashing.

Steel met steel in a shower of sparks. Hollister managed to parry Tom's first slash at his head, rolling the blade to his right and away from his body. Tom tried to reverse his direction, rolling his wrist slightly, and came up under Hollister's sword arm, cutting into the exposed armpit. His tactic failed as Hollister made an attack of his own.

The heavy cavalry sabre swung inward, raking strips of bone and wood from the flared side of Tanaka Tom's helmet, causing Tom's ears to ring with the force of the blow. He staggered, bumped into a rock and raised his *katana* barely in time to parry the next, skull-crushing attack aimed at the top of his head. Hollister was a good swordsman, that much he had to acknowledge. He hadn't learned that by hacking the helpless bodies of women and children. Of all the kills Tom meant to make to avenge his family, this one had to be right. He would use only naked steel. He holstered the Colt revolver and drew the short, *ho-tachi* sword, making a fast swipe at Hollister's open right side.

Jumping back quickly, Hollister managed to avoid the perilous blow. The wounds of screaming horses, yelling men, and nearly endless gunshots added to the confusion. He now faced two swords and realized the danger he found himself in. Hollister's left hand stole to the butt of a Hopkins and Allen five shot .31 revolver tucked backward in his belt. Behind him, the fury of battle increased to a crescendo and suddenly half a dozen frenzied, eye-rolling harness horses broke out of the compound and charged down upon the two men.

They leaped backward to safety in the same instant, dust swirling up to hide each from the other's sight. When the air cleared, Tanaka Tom could see nothing of Hollister. The press of action surged toward him again and he spun, drawing his Colt, to dispatch one outlaw who tried to leap on him from behind. In the distance he heard a calm voice giving orders, rallying Hollister's troops.

Rushing among the disorganized outlaws, Pike Turner gave an encouraging word here, fired a covering shot there. He reached the spot where several men worked to harness teams to the wagons. All the while, his mind swarmed with questions. How had this one man turned into a small army? Who exactly was

Fletcher and what did he want with them? No time for speculation now. He reached out to Phil Danvers, the man Hollister designated quartermaster sergeant, and took him by the arm.

"Phil . . . got to get us moving out of here. Don't fool with any wagons beyond these three. That takes care of the money, guns, ammunition, and food supplies for the march. Hurry!" At Danvers's nod, Turner moved off to organize some sort of rear-guard action. He looked up to see Edward Hollister heading his way, struggling through the milling horses. He changed directions, meeting the colonel in the shelter of a high-sided wagon.

"Dammit, Captain Turner, you'd think these men had never been under fire before. Get your troops organized into a rear guard and let's make ready to get out of here."

"Already in progress, sir. I was on my way to see to the rear guard."

Far from satisfied, Edward Hollister compressed his lips to a thin, disapproving line. "At least someone has kept his wits about him."

"Yes, sir. The three wagons over there contain all that is absolutely necessary for us to take along. I'd suggest you wait over there."

"Very good, captain. Carry on." Hollister all but saluted.

Tanaka Tom ran headlong into Turner's rear-guard action. One moment he faced a single man, two pistols blazing at the same instant. The outlaw spun away with a painful cry. Then seven men closed in on the young samurai. Reduced by the ferocity of the battle to using their rifle and carbine stocks like clubs—no one had opened reserve ammunition supplies—they had presence of mind to arm themselves with other things as well.

A large blacksnake whip hissed through the air, snapping loudly as it contacted the hard, bone plates of Tom's helmet. Tom's thumb curled over the hammer of his Colt, earing it back, and when he let it drop, it fell on an empty chamber. Faced by so many adversaries, Tom felt a moment's loss, but met them with a samurai's implacable courage, planning as calmly their deaths . . . or his.

Chapter Eighteen

Presley Amis felt too terrified to run, but he wasn't all that sure about staying to fight. Who was this man with the long sword and a face like the wicked witch in the Punch and Judy stories he'd seen as a kid? The cowboys among the rocks he could understand. But this one, in the incredible costume . . . inhuman the way he faced seven of them without blinking an eye.

Then Presley Amis moved closer, holding his carbine at high port and wishing he had a bayonet like the one he'd run into the guts of those Johnny Rebs down in Georgia. Then he'd show this sword-wavin' jaspar a thing or two. In a flash, Amis realized that what he saw wasn't the man's face, but a remarkably realistic mask, the features painted on in snarling rage. Anyone who hid behind a mask like that couldn't have much in the way of grit, he thought confidently as he leaped forward. The butt of his weapon rose to smash the arrogant jaw. Presley hardly felt the pain when it first came. Sort of like being smacked on the arm by a teacher's ruler. He glanced down and the strength left his legs, toppling him as he shrieked in terror.

Bright blood pumped from the stumps of both forearms. Presley's horror came from the realization that he could never hope to staunch its flow without at least one hand to do the job. His sight dimmed and his hearing along with it, before the rest of the battle could be joined.

Tom Fletcher released his grip on the *katana* with his left hand, sending it to dip into the top of his *obi* as Amis's carbine and forearms fell to the ground. A succession of deadly *shuriken*, Gatling-gun fast, flashed through the air. The death stars clung, painful, and distracting where they didn't bite in well enough to incapacitate. As his attackers yelped and fell back, Tom unwound from around his waist the chain and hooked, sickle-bladed warhead of a *kusarigama*.

The deeply curved, steel blade whistled through the air, propelled by the strength of Tanaka Tom's arm and the weight of the chain. Its tip caught in flesh, digging in, then slicing out as Tom flicked his wrist, disemboweling one gunslinger. Anorther of Hollister's soldiers charged it, using his rifle to block. In theory his plan worked. In practice it became a disaster.

The steel barrel and wooden forestock of his Henry stopped the chain all right. Then, whipping on its inexorable course, the *kusarigama* crescent bit into his back, cutting deeply, destroying one kidney before a strong jerk from Tanaka Tom brought it out the man's side, spilling blood and intestines in its wake. Reversing his left forearm and wrist, Tom employed a lashing, serpentine movement to the stout length of chain, driving the outlaws, cowering, before him. When one tripped over a sprawled corpse, Tom's *katana* flashed and the gunhawk died as the stroke cleaved his chest to the spine. Suddenly the rear guard broke and ran.

A few stray shots followed from the cowboys among the rocks, under Abe Barton's command. Then silence. A distant pounding of hoofs. A moan from a wounded man. Mostly, though, the silence. Tanaka Tom strode into the center of the clearing, idly wiping blood off his weapons on the shirt of one of his victims. The others stood among the rocks, revealing themselves for the first time. Tom called to Abe.

"Better signal that boy of yours to bring up the horses. We have a long ride to catch up to those who got away."

"What do you mean catch up to them? We killed a dozen, maybe fifteen men here. Lost three of our own. Ain't that enough?"

"No, Mr. Barton. Edward Hollister and Pike Turner escaped us. They took three wagons with them. It doesn't take any great intelligence to realize that the ones they chose contained what they would need to outfit another small army like this. I want Hollister. You and your men agreed to fight this my way. Get the horses, we ride after them."

Turning back to glance over his shoulder, Edward Hollister, who sat astride his blooded Arabian, motioned to Pike Turner. The outlaw joined him.

"I don't hear any more firing."

"At this distance, the wagon wheels would drown it out, Colonel. Those are good men back there. I picked them myself."

"If they are so damn good, why are we running away like whining cowards? Dammit, Captain, I don't like this one bit. A force of twenty-five and we get away with only five. From now on, Captain, until you can field a more effective force, I shall conduct operations from headquarters."

"You're going back to Denver, then, sir?"

"Yes. Without men and equipment, the Mexican project is, at least temporarily, out of the question. I have a few matters to attend to, ah . . . elsewhere. When they are concluded, I will go to Denver. In the meanwhile, I want you to take your best . . . if such a word can be applied in this case . . . men and find this . . . this . . . what did you say his name was?"

"Fletcher, sir."

"Yes. Find Fletcher and eliminate him. If the time and place are right, get from him why he came after us. If not, simply dispose of him."

"I'll do as you say, sir."

"Let's ride on, then. Ruiz will be waiting."

"They're there! The wagons. Right over this rise!" Reining in his heaving mount, green-tinged foam flying in streams from the animal's mouth, Lorry Garnett pointed behind him, emphasizing his shouted announcement.

"All right, men. We'll be on top of them in no time. When we go over that crest, fan out, and keep the center deeper than the wings. Ride down in a crescent-shaped formation so that none of them can break to the sides and escape. As soon as the center closes with the wagons, swing in from the right and left and we'll have them trapped." Drawing his *katana*, Tom Fletcher urged his weary Morgan into a gallop.

Topping the rise and looking to the south, Tom saw that they would close to rifle range in a matter of moments. Letting his gaze go beyond the fleeing wagons, he saw a second long plume of dust rising, growing nearer. What could this be? Waving his *katana* over his head, he gave his small force the signal to charge.

Rapidly they neared the enemy. A rifle crashed close to Tom's ear, answered immediately by two men lying in the jolting box of the rearmost wagon. The shots grew to be a volley as more of his force swung out into line to close in on the fleeing Hollister and his men. Then, suddenly, Abe Barton reined up, waving his hands wildly, jolting the others to halt. Anger flashed through Tanaka Tom as he rode to the older man.

"What are you stopping for? We nearly had them."

In the near distance, the wagons labored up a small swell and lumbered past a group of mounted men. Barton shook a helpless finger at the departing outlaws.

"That's Mexico over there. And those is *Federales*. If they don't want us to go on, they'll stop us with bullets."

No sooner had Barton spoken than Tom saw Edward Hollister ride to a place beside the officer at the head of the gaudily uniformed *soldados*. Hollister took a large, leather pouch from an inner coat pocket. He made an elaborate gesture of handing it to the *capitán*, who in turn made an equally ostentatious display of accepting it. The men shook hands and Hollister rode to the head of his small column. Behind him, between the outlaws and Tom's vengeance-bound command, the *Federales* drew their carbines on a command from their leader.

"By God, he bought 'em off!" Abe Barton shouted. "We better make tracks."

A volley, inaccurate and ill-aimed, buzzed angrily

154

over their heads. Fierce anger flickered hotly in Tom Fletcher's breast as he had to sit helplessly and watch his arch enemy ride to safety beyond the covering guns of the Mexican troops. Reluctantly, accepting the wisdom of Barton's words as his karma, he turned the Morgan's head northward and led his cowboy volunteers out of range.

EPILOGUE

In a small *cantina*, on the outskirts of Tucson, Tom Fletcher sat at a rear table. A small inkpot rested on the rough, wooden surface before him and his left hand held a slender, bamboo shaft with a shaped brush at one end. His attention was on the sheet of paper that lay between his arms, not on the scantily clad women or rough-dressed men at the bar. Sighing heavily, he dipped the brush into ink and began to write. The calligraphic characters of Japanese flowed evenly onto the off-white foolscap.

"Honored Father. I have encountered the enemy and eliminated several responsible for the dishonor of my family. I have even confronted the infamous Colonel Edward Hollister. It is to my dishonor that I failed to avenge my shame with his blood. Hollister is a far more powerful man, with considerably greater wealth than we first believed. His resources and influence spread over much of this country, which seems so strange to me.

"America is a large nation, far bigger than we of Nippon believed. It rivals the so-called civilized portion of *Katchin* and travel is time consuming. My quest, therefore, shall take many more months than expected. Although Hollister escaped me, the tentacles of his organization extend everywhere. Sooner or later I shall encounter him again. Now I make plans to seek out yet another of his minions.

"It is said, by General Tomlinson, that this man has recently been appointed to a post in the government. He serves as an agent on an Indian reservation within this very territory, Arizona, from which I write this unhappy letter. His position, both the general and I believe, was obtained by Hollister's influence."

Tom Fletcher looked up from the page. How could he explain it? What could he say about the strange feeling of duality that now grew within him? That part of him that was of the West seemed each day to assert itself more and more, yet he felt so totally of the East. He shrugged off the thought. If his karma permitted it he would find Edward Hollister and bring down vengeance upon him as his honorable ancestors demanded . . . not in the way of an occidental, but as a samurai. *Banzai!*

GLOSSARY

JAPANESE

Age uke—Rising forearm block.

Ainu—Caucasian-like Japanese inhabiting the northern area of the Asian country.

Amerika-jin—American (person).

Anata-no-onamae wa?—"What is your name?"

Bajutsu—Samurai horsemanship.

Banzai—"Ten thousand years," a battle cry.

Biru—Beer.

Butai—Detachment.

Buton—A candy made of rice, sugar, and plum syrup.

Cha—Green tea.

Chichi—Father.

Daimyo—Japanese warlord.

Dai Nippon—Japan.

Daisho—Traditional long and short sword set of the samurai.

Dom arigato—Thank you.

Ebira—Archer's quiver.

Edo—Tokyo.

Eeya—No.

Fumikomi—Front 'stamp' kick.

Furi-zuk—A wedge hand blow used in *Shorinji Kempo Karate*.

Gehtas—Wooden sandals.

Gi—A uniform worn for martial arts practice.

Gohon—Boiled rice.

Go-shan—Brothel.

Hai—Yes.

Ho-tachi—Samuari short sword.

158

Ichi—One.

Ichi-do—"On guard" sword position or *kamae*.

Juji-uke—'A' or 'X' block, using crossed arms at the wrists to stop a blow or kick.

Kaki—Oysters.

Kamakazi—"Divine wind." A typhoon.

Karma—One's individual destiny according to Zen.

Karate—"Empty hand," a martial art using one's body as a weapon.

Kasoku-tei—Heel kick.

Kata—A method of practicing a series of karate techniques in a dance-like manner.

Katana—Samurai long sword.

Ken tsui—Hammer fist, striking with the bottom of the fist.

Ki—Inner strength, unites mind and spirit with body.

Kiayi—A karate shout, also called '*kiai*' and '*kiya*.'

Kiku-san—"Little sir."

Kimono—A buttonless jacket or robe.

Kusarigama—Chain weapon with an iron ball attached to one end and a sickle to the other.

Kyujutsu—Samurai combat archery.

Mae geri keage—Front snap kick.

Mikkado—Emperor. Considered a divine personage, he did not conduct himself with government or ruling the people.

Musuko—Son.

Nakazashi—War arrow.

Ninja—Member of a society of espionage agents and assassins.

Obi—Sash.

Ohayō—Good morning.

Rentai—Regiment

Ronin—A samurai without a master, generally a mercenary.

Samurai—A warrior-knight of Japan.

San—"Sir" or "mister."

Sei-etei—Most powerful lord of the land.

Seppuku—Ritual of suicide by disembowelment to compensate for dishonor. Often incorrectly called *hira-kiri*.

Shinto—A religion that holds natural forces and imperial ancestors in reverence. Once the state religion of Japan.

Shōgun—The defacto leader of the government of Japan. The supreme military head and prime minister. Traditionally, a military governor who enforced a quasi-dynasty of absolute rule.

Shuriken—A spike or star-shaped weapon thrown at an opponent. The skilled use of these objects is called *Shuriken-jutsu*.

Shuto—A karate blow with the side of the hand.

Sumo—A traditional form of wrestling.

Tabi—A split-toed slipper.

Tanto—Samurai knife.

Teisho—Heel of the palm blow.

Tobi geri—Leap kick.

Tomoe-nage—The 'circle' throw.

Tonki—Small throwing weapons, including *shurikens*.

Ura ken—Back fist blow.

Ushiro hiji ate—Backward elbow smash.

Wakarimasu desu?—Do you understand?

Yasai tenpura no tomo—Fried vegetables.

Yoko geri keage—Side kick.

Yoko hiji ate—Sideways elbow smash.

Yon hon nukite—Spearhead blow, using the tips of one's stiffened fingers to strike an opponent's vital areas.

SPANISH

Ajo—Garlic.

Ándale—Hurry.

Bandido—Bandit.

Borrego—Sheep.

Burro—Donkey.

Caballos—Horses.

Cantina—Saloon.

Carne—Meat. *Carne de res*—beef.

Cerveza—Beer.

Comidas—Meal.

De nada—"It is nothing," you're welcome.

Español—Spanish.

Estúpido—Stupid.

Federales—Mexican troops serving as federal police.

Habla—Speak.

Huaraches—Thick-soled, Mexican leather sandals.

Indio—Indian.

Ingles—English.

Loco—Crazy.

Lonchería—Lunch counter.

Malos—Bad (plural).

Mande—"Hand it to me" or say it again.

Mariachi—Traditional Mexican strolling troubadours, usually consisting of three guitars, two trumpets and a violin.

Mira—Look.

Momentito—"Just a second."

No intiendo—"I do not understand."

Por—For.

Por favor—"For a favor," please.

¿Por que no?—"Why not?"

¡Que la chigada!—"Oh, fuck!"

Rancheria—Ranch.

Señor (es)—Sir or gentleman. Gentleman in plural.

Sí—Yes.

Siesta—Afternoon nap in Latin American countries.

Soldados—Soldiers.

Sombrero—Hat.

Sombrero de Corta—Low, flat-crowned ranch owner's hat, most frequently worn by *matadors* as part of their street clothing, and those fighting bulls in the Portuguese-style, on horseback.

Tortillas—Flat bread cakes made of corn or wheat flour baked on a hot iron plate.

Usted—You.

**Out of the American West rides a new hero.
He rides alone . . . trusting no one.**

SPECIAL PREVIEW

EDGE

BY

George G. Gilman

*Edge is not like other western novels. In a tradition-bound
genre long dominated by the heroic cowpoke, we now have
the western anti-hero, an un-hero . . . a character seemingly
devoid of any sympathetic virtues. "A mean, sub-bitchin,'
baad-ass!" For readers who were introduced to the western via
Fran Striker's Lone Ranger tales, and who have learned about
the ways of the American West from the countless volumes
penned by Max Brand and Zane Grey, the adventures of Edge
will be quite shocking. Without question, these are the most
violent and bloody stories ever written in this field. Only two
things are certain about Edge: first, he is totally unpredicta-
ble, and has no pretense of ethics or honor . . . for him there
is no Code of the West, no Rules of the Range. Secondly, since
the first book of Edge's adventures was published by Pinnacle
in July of 1972, the sales and reader reaction have continued
to grow steadily. Edge is now a major part of the western
genre, alongside ol' Max and Zane, and Louis L'Amour. But*

Edge *will never be confused with any of 'em, because* Edge *is an original, tough hombre who defies any attempt to be cleaned up, calmed-down or made honorable. And who is to say that* Edge *may not be a realistic portrayal of our early American West? Perhaps more authentic than we know.*

George G. Gilman created *Edge* in 1971. The idea grew out of an editorial meeting in a London pub. It was, obviously, a fortunate blending of concepts between writer and editor. Up to this point Mr. Gilman's career included stints as a newspaperman, short story writer, compiler of crossword puzzles, and a few not-too-successful mysteries and police novels. With the publication in England of his first *Edge* novel, *The Loner*, Mr. Gilman's writing career took off. British readers went crazy over them, likening them to the "spaghetti westerns" of Clint Eastwood. In October, 1971, an American editor visiting the offices of New English Library in London spotted the cover of the first book on a bulletin board and asked about it. He was told it was "A cheeky Britisher's incredibly gory attempt at developing a new western series." Within a few days Pinnacle's editor had bought the series for publication in the United States. "It was," he said, "the perfect answer to the staid old westerns, which are so dull, so predictable, and so all-alike."

The first reactions to *Edge* in New York were incredulous. "Too violent!" "It's too far from the western formula, fans won't accept it." "How the hell can a British writer write about *our* American West?" But Pinnacle's editors felt they had something hot, and that the reading public was ready for it. So they published the first two *Edge* books simultaneously; *The Loner* and *Ten Grand* were issued in July 1972.

But, just *who* is Edge? We'll try to explain. His name was Josiah Hedges, a rather nondescript, even innocent, monicker for the times. Actually we meet Josiah's younger brother, Jamie Hedges, first. It is 1865, in the state of Iowa, a peaceful farmstead. The Civil War is over and young Jamie is awaiting the return of his brother, who's been five years at war. Six hundred thousand others have died, but Josiah was coming home. All would be well again. Jamie could hardly contain his excitement. He wasn't yet nineteen.

The following is an edited version of the first few chapters, as we are introduced to Josiah Hedges:

* * *

Six riders appeared in the distance, it must be Josiah! But then Jamie saw something which clouded his face, caused him to reach down and press Patch's head against his leg, giving or seeking assurance.

"Hi there, boy, you must be Joe's little brother Jamie."

He was big and mean-looking and, even though he smiled as he spoke, his crooked and tobacco-browned teeth gave his face an evil cast. But Jamie was old enough to know not to trust first impressions: and the mention of his brother's name raised the flames of excitement again.

"You know Joe? I'm expecting him. Where is he?"

"Well, boy," he drawled, shuffling his feet. "Hell, when you got bad news to give, tell it quick is how I look at things. Joe won't be coming today. Not any day. He's dead, boy."

"We didn't only come to give you the news, boy," the sergeant said. "Hardly like to bring up another matter, but you're almost a man now. Probably are a man in everything except years—living out here alone in the wilderness like you do. It's money, boy.

"Joe died in debt, you see. He didn't play much poker, but when he did there was just no stopping him."

Liar, Jamie wanted to scream at them. *Filthy rotten liar*.

"Night before he died," the sergeant continued. "Joe owed me five hundred dollars. He wanted to play me double or nothing. I didn't want to, but your brother was sure a stubborn cuss when he wanted to be."

Joe never gambled. Ma and Pa taught us both good.

"So we played a hand and Joe was unlucky." His gaze continued to be locked on Jamie's, while his discolored teeth were shown in another parody of a smile. "I wasn't worried none about the debt, boy. See, Joe told me he'd been sending money home to you regular like."

"There ain't no money on the place and you're a lying sonofabitch. Joe never gambled. Every cent he earned went into a bank so we could do things with this place. Big things. I don't even believe Joe's dead. Get off our land."

Jamie was held erect against this oak, secured by a length of rope that bound him tightly at ankles, thighs, stomach, chest, and throat; except for his right arm left free of the bonds so that it could be raised out and the hand fastened, fingers splayed over the tree trunk by nails driven between them and bent over. But Jamie gritted his teeth and looked back at Forrest defiantly, trying desperately to conceal the twisted terror that reached his very nerve ends.

"You got your fingers and a thumb on that right hand, boy," Forrest said softly. "You also got another hand and we got lots of nails. I'll start with the thumb. I'm good. That's why they made me platoon sergeant. Your brother recommended me, boy. I don't miss. Where's the money?"

The enormous gun roared and Jamie could no longer feel anything in his right hand. But Forrest's aim was true and when the boy looked down it was just his thumb that lay in the dust, the shattered bone gleaming white against the scarlet blood pumping from the still warm flesh. Then the numbness went and white hot pain engulfed his entire arm as he screamed.

"You tell me where the money is hid, boy," Forrest said, having to raise his voice and make himself heard above the sounds of agony, but still empty of emotion.

The gun exploded into sound again and this time there was no moment of numbness as Jamie's forefinger fell to the ground.

"Don't hog it all yourself, Frank," Billy Seward shouted, drawing his revolver. "You weren't the only crack shot in the whole damn war."

"You stupid bastard," Forrest yelled as he spun around. "Don't kill him. . . ."

But the man with the whiskey bottle suddenly fired from the hip, the bullet whining past Forrest's shoulder to hit Jamie squarely between the eyes, the blood spurting from the fatal wound like red mud to mask the boy's death agony. The gasps of the other men told Forrest it was over and his Colt spoke again, the bullet smashing into the drunken man's groin. He went down hard into a sitting position, dropping his gun, splaying his legs, his hands clenching at his lower abdomen.

"Help me, Frank, my guts are running out. I didn't mean to kill him."

"But you did," Forrest said, spat full into his face and brought up his foot to kick the injured man savagely on the jaw, sending him sprawling on to his back. He looked around at the others as, their faces depicting fear, they holstered their guns. "Burn the place to the ground," he ordered with low-key fury. "If we can't get the money, Captain damn Josiah C. Hedges ain't gonna find it, either."

Joe caught his first sight of the farm and was sure it was a trick of his imagination that painted the picture hanging before his eyes. But then the gentle breeze that had been coming from the south suddenly veered and he caught the acrid stench of smoke in his nostrils, confirming that the black smudges rising lazily upwards from the wide area of darkened country ahead was actual evidence of a fire.

As he galloped toward what was now the charred remains of the Hedges farmstead, Joe looked down at the rail, recognizing in the thick dust of a long hot summer signs of the recent passage of many horses—horses with shod hoofs. As he thundered up the final length of the trail, Joe saw only two areas of movement, one around the big oak and another some yards distant, toward the smouldering ruins of the house, and as he reined his horse at the gateway he slid the twelve shot Henry repeater from its boot and leapt to the ground, firing from hip level. Only one of the evil buzz that had been tearing ferociously at dead human flesh escaped, lumbering with incensed screeches into the acrid air.

For perhaps a minute Joe stood unmoving, looking at Jamie bound to the tree. He knew it was his brother, even though his face was unrecognizable where the scavengers had ripped the flesh to the bone. He saw the right hand picked almost completely clean of flesh, as a three fingered skeleton of what it had been, still securely nailed to the tree. He took hold of Jamie's shirt front and ripped it, pressed his lips against the cold, waxy flesh of his brother's chest, letting his grief escape, not moving until his throat was pained by dry sobs and his tears were exhausted. . . .

"Jamie, our ma and pa taught us a lot out of the Good Book, but it's a long time since I felt the need to know about such things. I guess you'd know better than me what to say at a time like this. Rest easy, brother, I'll settle your score. Whoever they are and wherever they run, I'll find them and I'll kill them. I've learned some special ways of killing people and I'll avenge you good." Now Joe looked up at the sky, a bright sheet of azure cleared of smoke. "Take care of my kid brother, Lord," he said softly, and put on his hat with a gesture of finality, marking the end of his moments of graveside reverence. Then he went to the pile of blackened timber which was the corner of what had been Jamie's bedroom. Joe used the edge of the spade to prise up the scorched floor boards. Beneath was a tin box containing every cent of the two thousand dollars Joe had sent home from the war, stacked neatly in piles of one, five, and ten dollar bills.

Only now, more than two hours since he had returned to the farmstead, did Joe cross to look at the second dead man

The scavenging birds had again made their feast at the man-made source of blood. The dead man lay on his back, arms and legs splayed. Above the waist and below the thighs he was unmarked, the birds content to tear away his genitals and rip a gaping hole in his stomach, their talons and bills delving inside to drag out the intestines, the uneaten portions of which now trailed in the dust. . . .

Then Joe looked at the face of the dead man and his cold eyes narrowed. The man was Bob Rhett, he recalled. He had fought a drunken coward's war, his many failings covered by his platoon sergeant Frank Forrest. So they were the five men who must die . . . Frank Forrest, Billy Seward, John Scott, Hal Douglas, and Roger Bell. They were inseparable throughout the war.

Joe walked to his horse and mounted. He had not gone fifty yards before he saw a buzzard swoop down and tug at something that suddenly came free. Then it rose into the air with an ungainly flapping of wings, to find a safer place to enjoy its prize. As it wheeled away, Joe saw that swinging from its bill were the entrails of Bob Rhett.

Joe grinned for the first time that day, an expression of cold slit eyes and bared teeth that utterly lacked humor. "You never did have any guts, Rhett," he said aloud.

* * *

From this day of horror Josiah Hedges forged a new career as a killer. A killer of the worst kind, born of violence, driven by revenge. As you'll note in the preceding material, Edge often shows his grim sense of irony, a graveyard humor. Edge is not like anyone you've met in fact or fiction. He is without doubt the most cold-bloodedly violent character to ever roam the West. You'll hate him, you'll cringe at what he does, you'll wince at the explicit description of all that transpires . . . and you'll come back for more.